WE COULD BE
HEROES

WE COULD BE
HEROES

Margaret Finnegan

 Atheneum Books for Young Readers
New York London Toronto Sydney New Delhi

ATHENEUM BOOKS FOR YOUNG READERS
An imprint of Simon & Schuster Children's Publishing Division
1230 Avenue of the Americas, New York, New York 10020

For information about special discounts for bulk purchases, please contact Simon & Schuster Special Sales at 1-866-506-1949 or business@simonandschuster.com.
The Simon & Schuster Speakers Bureau can bring authors to your live event. For more information or to book an event, contact the Simon & Schuster Speakers Bureau at 1-866-248-3049 or visit our website at www.simonspeakers.com.
Book design by Karyn Lee
The text for this book was set in Amasis MT.
Manufactured in the United States of America
0120 FFG
First Edition
2 4 6 8 10 9 7 5 3 1
Library of Congress Cataloging-in-Publication Data
Names: Finnegan, Margaret Mary, 1965– author.
Title: We could be heroes / Margaret Finnegan.
Description: First edition. | New York : Atheneum Books for Young Readers, [2020] | Summary: Fourth graders Maisie and Hank, who has autism, become friends as they devise schemes to save a neighbor's dog, Booler, from being tied to a tree because of his epilepsy.
Identifiers: LCCN 2019006544 | ISBN 9781534445253 (hardcover) | ISBN 9781534445277 (eBook)
Subjects: | CYAC: Friendship—Fiction. | Autism—Fiction. | Dogs—Fiction. | Epilepsy—Fiction. | Family life—Fiction. | Schools—Fiction.
Classification: LCC PZ7.1.F53684 We 2020 | DDC [Fic]—dc23
LC record available at https://lccn.loc.gov/2019006544

To two real heroes: Elizabeth and Scout

Hank had things totally under control until he actually held up his brand-new Survival 4000 Fire Striker with Compass and Whistle—the one he got for his birthday, the one that he was only supposed to take camping—to Mrs. Vera's book. Then the unthinkable happened. The 495-page torture device that she had been reading to the class for the last week—the one he had begged her to put away, the one about the thin, starving, scared boy who would most certainly be killed by Nazis—would not burn. Maybe it was the hard cover. Maybe the boys' bathroom, where Hank stood committing his crime of passion, repelled fire. Maybe his mom was right after all: You never, *ever, ever, ever* burn books. Whatever it was, the paper merely ruffled and let off a little smoke.

Worry set in. He only had a few minutes of lunch left, and if he didn't get the job done now, he'd be forced to suffer another afternoon with that terrible, terrible book. But that was when all those weekends of roughing it with his family in the Montana wilderness paid off. Because Hank knew that fires need kindling, and do you know what makes good kindling? Paper towels. Hank took all of them from the dispenser and spread them into a little pile on the ground. Then, like he was returning a precious dragon's egg to its nest, he settled the book on top of the paper towels. He picked up his fire striker. He slammed the stainless steel rod against the magnesium-coated bar and watched as a spark smoldered on the paper towels and then erupted into flames.

Hank took a step back. The fire began to eat away at the paper towels and then at the book. Relief settled over him and his whole body felt lighter. Finally, he was free. He was free of the story. He was free of the boy. He was free of all the fourth graders seeing him cry every time the Nazi soldiers made the boy's sad and scary life even sadder and scarier.

But then the smoke detector went off. And the sprinklers on the ceiling sprouted water. And Hank thought maybe it was time to leave.

Here, Hank got lucky. He slipped out of the bathroom and grabbed his down coat from the empty classroom before anyone saw him. Then—his hood covering his wet head—he walked all casual-like out of the building and over to the field. Of course no one noticed him then. No one ever noticed Hank. They didn't notice him enough to be friends with him. They didn't even notice him enough to be mean to him. And if they didn't notice him when things were regular, there was no way they would notice him with the fire alarm blaring across the field.

Students who only moments earlier had been poking at the pale lunch meats in their sandwiches were now scrambling onto the field, sorting themselves into long alphabetical lines, just like they had practiced during all those emergency drills. Hank, who even seven months into the school year had a hard time keeping his classmates straight, wandered to the end of his line and tried to look cool.

The new girl—the one who had moved to Meadowlark a few months ago—hollered, "Up here, Hank. You need to be up here."

"Up there, Hank," repeated the boy in front of Hank. "You need to stand behind Maisie. Hudson goes after Huang."

Hank crunched through the dusting of snow that sparkled on the brown and muddy field. He saw Maisie watching him and lowered his gaze.

"I wonder if there's really a fire or if this is just a drill," said Maisie, bubbly and excited. She was taller than him and had black hair that grazed her chin. Despite the spring snowstorm that had snuck up on everyone in the night, she wore a thin pink coat and red plastic rain boots. Hank used to have boots like them and he had always liked the squelching sound they made when he moved through mud. His heart gave a hiccup as he wondered what had ever happened to those boots.

Maisie shuffled left and right to better see around the lines of students. "I think maybe it's a real fire because I've never seen a drill during recess. Have you?"

"Shhh. I'm listening to your shoes."

She turned around and peered at him. "You're listening to my shoes? That's the strangest thing I've ever heard." Her eyes narrowing, she added, "Hey, how come you're wet?"

Hank looked away.

She stepped back and scanned his whole body, her head moving up and down. "Your bangs are wet and your pants and shoes are wet too."

"I . . . um . . . Stop talking to me."

When Maisie didn't answer, Hank slid his eyes over to find her staring straight at him, her lips squeezed tight. His insides went cold and he looked away again. He slipped his hand in his pants pocket and grasped his three rocks of the day—carefully chosen, as usual, from his rocks and minerals collection.

He whispered the names of the rocks—"unakite, feldspar, augite"—to distract him from the weight of Maisie's stare.

"I got my eye on you," she said, changing from bubbly to dangerous with that one little phrase.

Hank turned sideways and his shoulders gave a small shudder. He did not like the idea of Maisie's eye on him.

A fire truck came.

And then another.

And then some firefighters in fluorescent jackets that shouted yellow came in the yard and the principal went and talked to them. Hank saw them hand her something. It was a very soggy book with a charred cover. He saw the principal hold the dripping book out in front of her like it was a stinking fish on a hook. Then Mrs. Vera shuffled over to the principal. The two women talked for a minute before they both looked over at Hank, who slowly pulled on the drawstring of his hood until all he could see was a wall of black.

"Oh, boy," said Maisie, her voice trumpeting through the cushioned padding of the hood. "You are in big trouble."

Hank was suspended for three days and grounded for five. But that wasn't the real punishment. The real punishment was that he had to return the Survival 4000 Fire Striker with Compass and Whistle to the grandparents who sent it to him. He also had to write them a letter explaining why he was undeserving of such a wonderful and practical device. Plus, he had to write letters of apology to his teacher, the principal, the firefighters, and even the custodians who had had to clean up the "giant mess he had created." Finally, he had to think carefully about his actions and endure countless stern looks and long lectures from his parents.

The last lecture had come the morning he was due to return to school. He had just chosen his rocks of the day from his rocks and minerals collection. The collection took up most of the space on the bookshelf in his room. The rest went to books about rocks and minerals. He looked at his bookshelf as his mom reminded him that he needed to make good choices, not start fires (a moot point since he'd had to give up his fire starter), and listen to his teacher, but to also be himself, and to always know that he was as good as anyone else, but that he definitely needed to respect his teacher and his principal.

"So let's hear it. What are the rules?" Mom asked him when she was finally done talking. She had the same dark hair and upturned nose as Hank, but her eyes were hazel, not the deep nutmeg that everyone said made Hank look like a deer.

She was holding Sam, who, at eleven months, permanently oozed drool. It occurred to Hank that the main good thing about going back to school was that he wouldn't have to witness those foot-long strands of spittle that dangled from his brother's slippery chin. But the very thought of school made Hank's hand tighten around the three rocks in his pocket. Today's beauties were rose quartz, gypsum, and pumice. The pumice was rough and light, and he suddenly wondered if his mom knew the very interesting fact that pumice floats.

He pulled the pumice from his pocket. "This is pumice. It

comes from volcanoes, and it is a very interesting fact that it floats," he said.

Mom shook her head. "What are the rules, Hank?"

The hand without the pumice gave a lazy swirl. The wrist went round and round as the fingers fanned out like spokes on a bicycle wheel. "No taking things that don't belong to me. No destroying other people's things."

"And?"

"No starting fires unless—"

"There is no unless. You may never start a fire—especially to burn a book, especially to burn a book about book-burning Nazis."

"How about when we go camping? Can I start a fire then? Dad always lets me start the campfire."

Mom's lips made a loud smacking sound that pained his ears. "Don't get technical with me. Until you hear otherwise, no starting fires. Ever." She slid Sam down onto her hip, where he turned his wet face and blinked at Hank.

"And?" she said.

Hank's hand began to swirl a little faster. He looked out his bedroom window. The snow from the other day had melted, and now, except for a few dirty banks of ice, things just looked muddy. "And I need to use my strategies when Mrs. Vera reads the book. I can pace in the back of the classroom. I can draw. . . . I can replay *Star Wars* in my head. . . ."

But the more Hank thought about what to do when Mrs. Vera read the book, the more he thought about the sad and scared boy, and the more he thought about the sad and scared boy, the more sad and scared Hank began to feel, and the more sad and scared Hank began to feel, the more *a'a* he began to feel.

A'a was a Hawaiian word Hank discovered in one of his rocks and minerals books. It described a kind of explosive lava flow where the lava moved and cooled at different rates. The top of the lava cooled faster than the bottom of the lava, which meant that on the surface the rock became rough and prickly and sharp, while on the bottom the rock became incredibly heavy and dense. *A'a* was how Hank felt when he had a meltdown. His world fell out of sync, like his body was moving at different rates. On the surface, everything became prickly and sharp. Sounds, textures, colors, smells poked him until he felt punctured and bruised. But even while that was happening, part of him felt heavy, dense, immovable. *A'a* was just like it sounded—two long awes signaling two awe-inspiring and simultaneous methods of destruction. *A'a* was the worst feeling ever. *A'a* was the thing he didn't like about having autism.

Mom lowered Sam to the floor. She wrapped Hank in a hug, and in a voice just louder than a whisper, she said, "I know it's hard for you to hear that book. I know it breaks you up inside just thinking of that little boy, but remember, that boy isn't real. It's just a story. And why do we listen to those kinds of stories?"

He sighed as the weight of her body made the *a'a* retreat. He said, "To make us sad."

His mother's chin dropped onto his shoulder. She took a deep breath. "No—well, yes—but only because it's important to get out of our own heads and know what other people's lives are, or were, like. Stories teach us empathy, to understand and care about how other people feel."

"I have empathy."

She ran her hand down his arm, and that wasn't *a'a* either. "You have lots of empathy, sweetheart. Maybe too much. But not everyone is like you."

Not for the first time, Hank wished that everyone could be more like him.

Hank walked the two blocks to school, and when he saw Mrs. Vera she greeted him with a funny little half grin that Hank could make no sense of at all.

"Well, look who is back," she said, one side of her mouth curled high above the other.

She was a piece of work, that Mrs. Vera. That's what his mother always said. Mrs. Vera was treelike—tall and thick-waisted with short, curly hair that sat atop her head like a nest. Plus, she dragged her left leg when she walked and she never explained why. She didn't even explain when Hank asked her why. She just gave him that little half grin and said, "Why, that is none of your business, Hank." Which always left Hank wondering one thing: Why was it none of his business when he saw her dragging her leg across the ground every day? And if Mrs. Vera offered a hug, it was not comforting and squishy at all. It was tree-trunk hard and wool-sweater scratchy.

At lunch, Hank sat at his usual empty cafeteria table, but his heart was on the field looking for rocks—the best rocks always turned up there once the snow melted—so he wolfed down his ham and cheese and ran to the back fence of the schoolyard. He was crouched down looking through some muddy gravel when Maisie's red boots appeared before him.

"Fess up," he heard her say. "Why'd you do it?"

"Do what?" It annoyed him that Maisie was distracting him from his important work.

"Why'd you burn down the bathroom?"

"It's not burned down. It just has water damage and maybe the beginnings of black mold. But my dad says that was probably already there."

Maisie dug the tip of her boot in the gravel, helpfully excavating a bunch of possibly important rocks. Hank raked a hand through the new finds.

"What did the bathroom ever do to *you* is what I'm asking," she said. "Are you, like, one of those wacky fire-loving kids or something?"

He had to think about that. He did like fire. He liked the way fires crackled and the way you could roast marshmallows and hot dogs over them. He liked that you got to sit around them and listen to your parents tell stories when you went camping. He had very much liked the Survival 4000 Fire Striker with Compass and Whistle and the way it almost seemed to chirp when the stainless steel rod hit the magnesium-covered bar. But he wouldn't say that he *loved* fire.

"I just wanted to get rid of that book Mrs. Vera reads to us. It's too sad."

"You risked burning down the whole school just because you don't like a book?" She sounded impressed. "That takes meatballs."

"No," Hank said with a shake of his head. "Just a fire striker. And paper towels." He stood and wiped his hands on his pants. Maisie's find was full of duds.

"I don't like that book either," she said, following Hank

as he moved to a new spot along the fence. "You know that boy is going to die. They always do."

Hank sighed. "Every time." He picked up an especially smooth and flat pebble, put it close to his face, and then slipped it in his pocket.

"What are you doing, anyhow?"

"I'm looking for rocks."

Maisie cocked her head, considering Hank more closely. "You like rocks?"

"I love rocks."

Maisie flipped her head the other way. "Huh," she mumbled. "I can work with that."

"What?"

"Listen." Maisie squatted next to Hank, getting closer than he would have liked. "I've got lots of rocks at home. Cool ones too. Big ones. We got this amethyst. It's so big we put a piece of glass on it and made it into a coffee table."

Hank's eyes widened.

Maisie picked up a handful of gravel and then poured it onto the ground through a loose fist. "Wanna come see?"

His mother could not stop smiling at Hank's father. They were sitting at the table eating dinner.

His father seemed confused.

"A girl from your class invited you to her house? This happened today?" said Dad. He was a freckly man with a reddish beard and bushy eyebrows that both awed Hank and left him strangely unsettled. His dad had on the hospital scrubs that he wore to his job as an emergency room nurse. The scrubs always awed and unsettled Hank too. Because what if those clothes had been near a bunch of sick people? Or bloody people? Or people with broken legs? It was a scary prospect, one that seemed to put Hank right in the middle of the emergency room. And Hank did not like the emergency room at all.

Dad asked him again, "Hank, a girl from your class invited you to her house? Really?"

"Yes," said Hank.

"And you want to go? Tomorrow?" The bushy eyebrows inched higher.

"Yes."

"And she likes rocks?" The bushy eyebrows almost touched his dad's hairline.

"She said she has lots of them."

And boy did she. Polished rocks—some as big as Hank's head—lay everywhere, and then of course there was the glass-topped amethyst coffee table. The enormous, bowl-like table base was a perfectly everyday-looking boulder on the outside and an explosion of craggy, purple gemstones on the inside. It was the most wonderful thing Hank had ever seen.

"That is a really big geode," marveled Hank, his nose almost touching the glass tabletop. "And it's a table. It's a rock *and* furniture—at the same time. This is the best house in the world. Or at least the country."

"It's because my parents are both geologists," she told Hank. "Those are professional rock experts. That's why we moved here. There's more going on here with rocks and stuff than where we lived in California."

She took him to the garage, which stood all by itself at the very back of her long yard, and showed him a whole closet full of rocks. Talk about treasure. Hank had never seen some of Maisie's rocks, even on his favorite rocks and minerals website.

"I'm gonna be a geologist too," said Hank, excited to be in the home of actual rocks and minerals professionals. "I have forty-six different types of rocks and minerals. I keep them on a special bookcase. My favorite is obsidian. Obsidian is an igneous rock—that means it's from a volcano. It's black, smooth, and shiny even without polishing. I have six pieces of obsidian. My second favorite—"

"Do you like dogs?" Maisie interrupted.

"They're okay. Mostly I like rocks. My second favorite—"

Maisie interrupted again. "I like dogs a lot. My neighbor has dogs. You want to meet them? They're really nice."

"No, I'd rather stay here." Hank stretched out a hand to touch a pointy pink stone unlike anything he had ever seen.

"We can see more rocks later," said Maisie, almost slamming the closet door on Hank's hand. "Come on."

Hank looked longingly at the closed closet door. But his mom had reminded him right before going to Maisie's house that sometimes you have to do what your friends want even if it's not what you want, so he apprehensively followed Maisie to the fence her family shared with their neighbor. It was a white wooden fence, about four feet high, with three long horizontal slats. Beyond the fence, under a large maple tree sprouting lime-green leaves, lay a sleeping dog.

"We can climb right over," Maisie said, lifting her feet one after the other onto the lowest slat and encouraging Hank to do the same. "My neighbor doesn't mind.

"Hey, Booler!" she called, jumping down from the top of the fence and into the other yard. The neighbor's yard was bigger than Maisie's, but that was because the house it belonged to was much smaller. In fact, it was tiny. It was rundown too, with peeling paint and one windowpane covered with wood. It was the kind of house that trick-or-treaters might shy away from, afraid that it could harbor ghosts or ghouls, but Maisie did not seem afraid, and so Hank was not afraid, just slightly alarmed.

Hank had not spent much time with animals, but he had seen his fair share of Animal Planet, and he could tell that the dog was a pit bull. It was almost entirely silver except for its neck and paws, which were white. It had a square face with almond-shaped eyes and a lolling, happy tongue.

"Why is it tied to the tree?" Hank asked.

Maisie sighed dramatically. "Isn't it awful?" she said as two other dogs bounded into the yard. One was big and black, the other small and golden. Hank guessed they were mutts. They rushed up to Maisie and nuzzled her with their snouts. When she squatted down they knocked her over and started licking her everywhere, making her laugh. The dog tied to the tree barked and jumped left and right with springlike legs that brought his whole body straight up in the air.

"Hey there, Cowboy," Maisie said, pulling herself up and petting the bigger mixed breed. "Hey there, Honey," she said to the smaller one. "This is Hank. He goes to my school."

Hank took a step forward. He put out his hands and the dogs gathered round to sniff them. He could not help but sniff the dogs back because the stench of them rose like a cloud and settled right around Hank's nose. They smelled of dirt and just a little bit of skunk. Still, their noses felt wet and cool against his skin and their whiskers tickled.

He smiled. "Nice doggies."

Behind them, the tied-up dog whined.

"Don't worry, you little cutie-pie," Maisie said, walking over to the other dog. "We haven't forgotten you. You're a good boy, aren't you?"

Hank and the other dogs followed Maisie, who, upon reaching the pit bull, knelt on one knee and ignored the mud seeping into her jeans. She pulled her face close and breathed him in. The dog sniffed Maisie in return and his muscles seemed to loosen. He let out a wobbly sigh and licked Maisie's chin.

"Hank, this is Booler," said Maisie.

Hank squatted next to Maisie. He took a hand and ran it across the dog's side, which was dusty and slick, and one whiff of him proved that he was even smellier than Cowboy and Honey combined.

Hank said, "Hey, boy."

"Booler's a good dog," said Maisie. "Cowboy and Honey are good too, but this guy is a big love." The pit bull dropped his head onto Maisie's knee and she began to scratch his scalp.

The other dogs circled round the tree, peed, and then began a loop around the backyard, stopping, sniffing, peeing with abandon at each plant and rock and even on the corner of the wooden doghouse nestled under the maple tree. Every once in a while they would come back to Maisie and Hank, demand affection, and then return to their pee-filled explorations.

"How come he's tied to the tree and the other dogs aren't?" Hank asked.

Maisie sighed even louder and more theatrically than before. "Well, it's a real disgrace. Booler started having seizures and Mr. Jorgensen—that's my neighbor, he's pretty old—says that Booler is just too much to handle now. You know what a seizure is?"

Hank opened his mouth to answer, but Maisie just continued on.

"Well," said Maisie, "there are these things called neurons in your brain, and they tell each other information, and sometimes, for some people—or dogs—they get too excited, and then your body has a seizure."

"And Booler has them?"

"Yep. He falls to the ground and shakes. And when you call his name he doesn't hear you at all, and when it's over he doesn't want to play. He just wants to sleep." She stroked Booler some more.

"Mr. Jorgensen says that tying Booler to the tree is the only way to keep him safe. But that's a load of hooey. You can see that it's just too lonely out here for Booler. Mr. Jorgensen only comes out to feed him. Cowboy and Honey come out sometimes, and they're nice and all, but—you see them—they want to play and run around. Poor Booler can only watch. I mean—look—that rope is probably only ten feet long. He gets so sad. He barks and whines. I hear him all the time. I come out here whenever I can, but you can see it's not enough.

"Plus, those seizures really scare Booler. They scare him so much that he can hardly breathe when he even thinks about them. He doesn't want to be all alone out here having a seizure. He wants to be with someone who loves him."

A hole was opening in Hank's chest. In his mind's eye he saw the dog, alone, sad, a tiny silver planet in a universe of blue velvet. No one to talk to. No mother to hug. No baby brother to kiss. Scared.

Hank could sense the *a'a* feeling taking over. And it wasn't just *his a'a*—it was like Booler's *a'a* was filling him up too. It was like he and Booler were watercolors. The dog's loneliness became Hank's loneliness. The dog's fear became Hank's fear. It was like the boy in the book all over again. Hank pulled out the three rocks from his pocket.

"This is slate," he said, holding the rock in front of the dog. "And look, this is chalk. You can use the chalk to write on the slate." He pulled the chalk across the slate, leaving a small white line.

"Booler is young," said Maisie. "He's only two years old. That's practically a puppy. He's got a whole life ahead of him! And he can do tricks. Watch."

She stood up. The dog stood too. "Sit, Booler."

The dog sat.

"Down, Booler."

The dog lay down.

"Shake, Booler." The dog offered a paw for Maisie to hold.

She turned to Hank. "And that's just a few of the things he can do. He is a very good watchdog. Whenever anyone comes down the street, Booler bolts up and barks his head off."

Hank's hand began to swirl. The pit bull was such a smart dog—such a smart, lonely, scared dog. It was too much. It was making him too sad. He tried to push down the *a'a*.

"I want to look at the rocks now," said Hank.

"In a minute," Maisie said, ignoring him for the third time that afternoon. "The thing is, Mr. Jorgensen doesn't really take care of Booler. You know who picks up the dog poop out here? Me. When I first started visiting Booler, dog poop was everywhere. It was poop-land-mine central. Booler hated it. It was stinky and gross. So I cleaned it up and I keep it clean. For Booler. It's pretty disgusting work too."

"It's still stinky," said Hank. "These dogs smell. A lot."

"That's because Mr. Jorgensen doesn't bathe them!" Maisie started counting off on her fingers. "He doesn't bathe them. He doesn't pick up their poop. He doesn't brush their teeth. He doesn't play with them. And those are all things you have to do if you have a dog! I know because I used to have a dog, but then she died because she got very old.

"I offered to take Booler off Mr. Jorgensen's hands, but—can you believe it?—he said no! He says Booler wouldn't want to live anywhere else and that Booler is fine with everything the way it is. Mr. Jorgensen is crazy stubborn."

Hank looked back at Maisie's house. The bubbling *a'a* reached behind his eyes. "You're making me sad."

"Hey! I have an idea!" Maisie said, a little too loudly and with a jarring snap of her fingers. "Why don't you take Booler? If we could get Booler to your house, he could live with you and Mr. Jorgensen would never know. Wouldn't that be great? I bet your family would be so happy to have such a great dog."

Hank blinked. He had already had to get used to a baby brother. Now a dog? Hank looked back at Booler. Booler was a nice dog. Booler was a sad dog, and seeing such a sad dog made Hank sad, but Hank was not a metamorphic rock. It was a very interesting fact that metamorphic rocks withstood high heat and pressure until they turned into a whole new kind of rock, but he could not have pebbles and sand and baby brothers and dogs globbing onto him, changing him, changing his world. His fingers folded around his rocks and his fist began to swirl.

"I don't have a dog."

"That's okay," Maisie assured him. "Booler will like being an only dog, and you can feed him, and give him a soapy bath, and he can sleep at the foot of your bed, and you can be best friends."

Hank shifted. His fist began to swirl more quickly. "I don't like to have things on the end of my bed when I sleep."

"It doesn't matter where Booler sleeps," Maisie said, her voice getting even louder. "You're missing the point. The point is that he would be happy because he would have a family he could really *be* with, and you would be happy because he is such a good dog and he would get to be *your* dog. And he wants to be your dog. I can tell."

Hank twisted round and looked at Maisie's house. "I . . . I . . . think Booler wants to be your dog."

Maisie rolled her eyes. "Well, of *course* he wants to be my dog, but Mr. Jorgensen says no. So now Booler wants to be your dog."

He leaned back, desperate. "Why me?"

"Well, Booler thinks you're pretty brave since you tried to burn down the school just because you hate a book. I told him all about it and he really gave me his big hopeful eyes when I was talking. He could tell you had the meatballs to save him. That's when I knew that Booler was counting on you to help him escape and to take care of him."

"I don't see how he could tell you—"

"I told you, he is very smart. He tells me a lot—with his face and stuff. Now, you've got to help Booler. He's counting on you."

Hank stood up. Both his arms were now hanging at his sides as his hands looped round and round at the wrists. "We don't have a dog. We have a baby. I think I should go home now." He ran back to the fence. His hands were gripping the wooden slats when Cowboy and Honey ran up and started nudging the back of his knees.

"No, no," he said. "Bad dogs."

"Don't call them bad dogs!" yelled Maisie. She was running toward him, her own hands balled in fists. "They just want to be your friends, like Booler. I'm telling you, Booler needs you!"

"I . . . I . . . I gotta go." Hank climbed over the fence. He wanted to run home but he wasn't sure which way to go, so he ran back to the garage instead. He couldn't even talk to Maisie when she found him. She was still yelling, standing over Hank flapping her hands around, but Hank didn't hear anything she was saying. He just sat there and stared at the rocks in the closet as he mumbled, "I was having a good day, but now it's a bad day. You gave me such a bad day, such a bad day."

Maisie stopped yelling and flapping. After a while she sat down next to Hank and began fidgeting with the laces on her shoe. Sounding a little like a frog, she said, "I just . . . thought you had the meatballs. I thought you'd want to help."

Hank shook his head. He stared at the rocks.

Maisie said nothing.

Their moms came.

"What's going on?" said Maisie's mom, who seemed like a grown-up version of Maisie. She had the same haircut, the same red boots, the same sunny voice that seemed ever ready to switch to dangerous.

"I didn't mean to break him," Maisie said guiltily.

"Maisie Huang, what did you do?" And there it was: dangerous.

"I'm sure it's fine," said Hank's mom, leaning down to rub

Hank's back. "Hank can be wound a little tight. It's not a good thing. It's not a bad thing. It's just what it is. Huh, Hank?"

Hank nodded. He said, "I was having a good day, but now it's a bad day."

He repeated the phrase again, and then again, and then again when they walked home.

Mom held his hand with one of her hands and pushed the baby stroller with her other. She didn't ask him what had happened. She didn't ask him why he was upset. Instead, when they were halfway to his house, she said, "So what rocks did you bring to school today?"

When he couldn't even tell her that, when he could only shake his head and mumble again, "I was having a good day, but now it's a bad day," she pulled some string cheese out of the diaper bag and gave it to him.

"Bad moments, even a lot of bad moments, don't make a day. What were the good parts of your day?"

But the good moments seemed so far away. They seemed so hard to remember. All he knew was that this was not a good moment. This was a bad moment, a moment that felt loud and sharp and heavy. He stopped walking and looked up at his mom. She knelt down and wrapped Hank in her arms. She squeezed and squeezed even when Sam started to chant, "Ma Ma Ma Ma Ma."

Then, without another word, they walked the rest of the way home. It wasn't that far really. Meadowlark was not much of a town, just a little place to shop and sleep on the way to the ski slopes at the top of the mountain behind it. It took about fifteen minutes to get from Maisie's to Hank's, but by the time they got home, the *a'a* feeling had lessened, and Hank, though tired, could at least tell his mom many amazing facts about his rocks, which was one of the good things he did like about his autism. He could reel off a lot of interesting facts about important things, like rocks.

When Dad got home, he said to Hank, "I hear your play-date was a bust, buddy. Well, you can't knock it out of the park every time."

"We didn't go to the park," said Hank. "We went to Maisie's."

"I see," said Dad. They were sitting on the couch watching Hank's favorite movie, *The Jungle Book*. Mom had put Sam to sleep so it was just the three of them lined up in a row. Hank was in the middle.

They watched *The Jungle Book* all the time, especially after bad days. It didn't have anything to do with rocks, but it was funny and Hank liked that. It was about a boy, Mowgli, raised by animals in the Indian jungle.

"You know," said Dad. "It wasn't always easy for Mowgli."

"Yeah," said Hank, barely paying attention because it was the part where Mowgli's best friend, Baloo the Bear, sang a funny song.

"But his pack looked out for him," said Dad.

"That's 'cuz his mom was a wolf," said Hank.

"Yeah. She had his back." Dad reached across the back of the couch and ran his fingers through Hank's mom's hair.

"We've got your back. You know that, right, Hank?" said Mom.

"Yeah," he said. He listened to Baloo sing and his mind drifted back to Maisie. It was really too bad she had given him a bad day. Because she had a lot of really cool rocks.

Hank was standing in line waiting for school to start. It was the day after his playdate with Maisie and he had come to school prepared. He had one goal: to keep Maisie from bringing up Booler. If she brought up Booler he would feel super sad, and if he felt super sad he would not be able to hold back the *a'a*. The only way to hold back the *a'a* was to avoid the things that awoke the *a'a*: disappointment, fear, sadness, uncertainty. And the best way to avoid those things was to stick with the familiar and predictable.

Of course, there was no guarantee she *would* bring up the dog.

His mom seemed pretty certain she would not. "Believe me," she'd said to him. "I'm sure Maisie has learned that that is not a good conversation for you two."

But Hank wasn't so sure. She seemed a little bit like a barnacle, that girl. He had a feeling that once she latched on to something, she would hold on forever. And so—of course—the need for a foolproof plan. And he had one! As soon as he saw Maisie approaching, he pulled a gigantic book, titled *Five Pounds of Fun Facts about Rocks and Minerals*, out of his backpack. He held it like it was no big deal, like he was just carrying it for absolutely no reason.

She said, "Hey."

"Hey," he said, turning away from her and looking out across the playground.

She moved in front of him. She seemed a little less enthusiastic than usual, which only made her motives more mysterious. "Um . . . I have lemon ricotta cookies in my lunch. I made them with my mom after you left. You want one?"

He thought she might be trying to trick him, but still, it was a cookie. He gave a brisk nod.

She took a cookie from her lunch bag and handed it to him. "They're really good."

He took a bite. They *were* really good.

She hesitated and then said, "So, you know that dog from yesterday? Booler?"

Ha! He'd been right! She *was* just like a barnacle! He set his foolproof plan into motion, but first he shoved the cookie right in his mouth because not even the best of plans were worth the sacrifice of a really good cookie. He chewed quickly as he flipped open the book. His mouth still full, he pointed to something on the page and said, "Yes, but did you know that according to *Five Pounds of Fun Facts about Rocks and Minerals* one of densest rocks on the planet is peridotite?"

She opened her mouth, but Hank barreled on. "You might be fascinated to know that diamonds are sometimes found in peridotite." He looked up, surveyed the situation.

She said, "But about—"

He looked back at the book. "You will also be fascinated to know that gabbro is another one of the world's most dense rocks."

Mrs. Vera came to walk them to class and saved Hank from having to regale Maisie with any more information. As they walked to class Hank watched the back of Maisie's hair swish from side to side. He smiled. He had always known that his facts would come in handy one day. He had always known.

Unfortunately, while Hank's plan was foolproof, he did not anticipate how long he would have to keep it up. And so he did not think to bring his book out to lunch. Big mistake. Maisie cornered him as he was looking for rocks—and she stepped right on all the good gravel too, so he couldn't ignore her.

"What are you doing?" she said.

He tried to think of an amazing fact. "Um . . . did you know that there are three kinds of rocks?"

She flipped back her hair. "Igneous. Sedimentary. Metamorphic. Duh. My parents are geologists."

Panicked, he tried to think of another fact, but this time she was too fast for him. She said, "So about Booler . . ."

Through clenched teeth, he said, "I don't want to hear about that dog."

She stepped closer. "I was just going to tell you—"

He looked past her and stared at the fence. "I'm not taking that dog."

She crossed her arms. "Jeez."

Hank began to rake through the gravel. He was determined to look everywhere except at Maisie.

She stepped right in front of him, waited a minute, and then cleared her throat. When he didn't look up she let out a bitter laugh. "Fine. I see how it is." She walked all around him, slowly, her hands behind her back. "Just so you know," she said when they faced each other once more, "you've broken Booler's heart."

He made a quarter turn. He said softly, "I'm not listening. I'm not listening. I'm not listening."

She moved in front of him again.

She began to speak like an actress in a movie so tragic that only grown-ups would ever want to see it. "When I visited Booler before school he was sprawled out on the ground and sighing. He didn't even pick his head up to say hi. He barely looked at me. He is super depressed."

Hank started to hum, but it was too late. He had heard her, and now his insides twisted as he imagined a depressed Booler. The worst part was that he had just *untwisted* his insides too. Mrs. Vera had been reading them that sad, sad book and it had taken him all morning to forget that the boy's father had up and disappeared, and the boy's grandparents were telling him he had to go hide in the woods despite the fact that they were too frail to go with him.

"Leave me alone," he demanded. "I'm trying to find rocks."

"I just can't see why you don't want Booler. There's something wrong with a kid who doesn't want the best dog in the world."

Hank's heart gave a hiccup. She had crossed a line. Oh, yes. She had crossed the mother of all lines. His eyes narrowed defiantly. He sat back on his heels and parroted what his mom always told him to say. "Nothing is wrong with me. Different is not less."

Maisie put her hands on her hips. "Well, any *normal* person would want Booler."

He felt his spine lengthen. He felt his neck stretch. He looked up to find her staring down at him, her eyebrows scrunched together and her face pale.

"I *am* normal," Hank hissed.

"Obviously not if you don't want Booler."

"I AM."

"NO, you're NOT!"

Hank lunged forward, fury erupting inside him. His hands found Maisie's legs and she fell backward.

A loud gasp escaped her mouth. "Oh, you did not just push me down." With a yell, she sprang forward and tackled Hank, pummeling his chest with her fists. Surprise replacing his rage, Hank pushed against her shoulders, and when that didn't stop her he turned onto his side and tried to shake her off, but that just relocated her punches from his chest to his back.

"Get. Off. Me!"

"Say you'll take Booler!"

"We already have a baby!"

Students began to gather round them. From narrowed eyes Hank spied shoes and pants jostling into one another. He heard voices, but the only words he could make out were "Hank," "Maisie," and "big trouble."

A shadow fell over Hank and he felt Maisie being lifted off

him. He peeked up to find Mrs. Vera scowling and breathing heavily. Her arms clutched a clawing, purple-faced Maisie.

Mrs. Vera shook her head. "What kind of behavior . . . fighting!" She grabbed them each by the shoulder and hauled them to the principal's office, depositing them on the couch in the reception area.

"Now what is going on here?" she asked, putting her hands on her hips in that way adults love to do.

Maisie turned away with a sneer.

Hank just shook his head. He had no idea where to start.

Mrs. Vera sighed. "I am very disappointed in you both, especially you, Hank. I thought you'd learned your lesson." Hank felt his face get hot. Mrs. Vera shuffled into the principal's office, her limp shaming them with a judging *shick*, *shick* sound. When she came out she squinted. Her mouth a prune, she said, "Stay," and headed back to class.

So they stayed. They stayed through the rest of recess. They stayed through the school receptionist helping some kid with a bloody nose. They stayed even when their mothers walked inside the building and gave them bitter frowns. Then they stayed while their moms talked to the principal without them.

"I was just looking for rocks," mumbled Hank.

"Well, I was just being my charming self."

A lump in his throat, he said, "It's charming to say people aren't normal?"

She screwed up her face and let loose an annoyed blast of air. "You know I didn't mean that." She paused, puffed up her chest, and added, "I gave you a cookie and everything."

He looked down. "It was a good cookie."

Maisie made a strange gurgling sound. She leaned toward Hank. "Look, I didn't mean to punch you or anything. I'm just worried about Booler."

He slid away from her, his hands giving a helpless flop. "Booler. I'm sick of hearing about Booler."

"Fine. I won't ever mention him again." Maisie crossed her arms and slid away from him too. She slid back. "But since we're on the subject, listen, you can't tell anybody about Booler."

Hank said nothing. He just stared down at his three rocks of the day (polished turquoise, rock salt, stinky sulfur).

"You can't tell, okay?"

"Oh, I'm gonna tell," he boomed. "You won't leave me alone about that dog."

The woman who guarded the principal's office looked over at them. She sniffed daintily as with one finger she pushed her glasses up the bridge of her nose.

Maisie slid her hands underneath her thighs and smiled

at the woman. When the woman looked back at her computer, Maisie swiveled toward Hank. She wiggled her hips and whispered right in Hank's ear, "If you tell them about Booler, then my parents will never let me visit him, because they already think I need to drop the subject before I drive them to an early grave."

"If they ask me what happened I'm gonna tell them what happened."

Maisie threw her hands upon her head and began to pull on the roots of her hair. Desperate, she said softly, "Okay, listen to me. You can have one of my parents' rocks."

Hank turned toward her, suspicious. "Which one?"

She dropped her hands onto her lap. "Not one of the ones in the house. My parents will notice that. One from the garage. Any one you want. Any one you can carry. Just let me do all the talking and don't disagree with me. Okay?"

The door to the principal's office opened. "Any one I can carry?" said Hank, who figured he could carry quite a lot.

"Yes! Just don't tell them about Booler."

Hank pinched his lips with his fingers. He did it all casual-like so no one would notice, with his elbows on his knees and his fingers gripping his mouth and his head bent low. But he did it. He didn't say a word about the dog. Not during the whole meeting. Not to the principal. Not to his mom. Not to Mrs. Huang. Not even when Maisie explained with velvety sweetness that they had been playing Jungle Book—Jungle Book! Instead, he thought as hard as he could about the apple-size amethyst that he had seen in Maisie's garage. It was not nearly as spectacular as the giant coffee-table amethyst, but it was still beautiful: purple and white and perfect. He was going to put it right on top of his dresser, the new showcase of his entire rock collection.

"You're telling me you were playing Jungle Book?" Hank's mom said. Her eyes were dubious pinpricks, her mouth a wavy line. When his bottom slid toward the front of his chair she reached out and squeezed his knee. "It's okay. You can tell us."

He thought harder about the dazzling gemstone that would soon be his.

Maisie said, "*The Jungle Book* is a very, very famous movie and also maybe a book because it has the word 'book' right in the title. I'm surprised you've never heard of it."

"Believe me, I *know* the movie," said Hank's mom, her eyes rolling to the top of her head.

"It's my favorite movie," said Hank, his eyes growing wide in surprise by the fingers that had abandoned his mouth so that the words could escape. He clamped down on his lips once more.

"It's my favorite movie too," said Maisie, sounding surprised herself. She regarded Hank for a moment and then went on. "So, yeah. We both love *The Jungle Book*. Jungle Book is our favorite game. Hank is always the boy, Mowgli, and I am always the bear, Baloo. Baloo was tickling Mowgli, not fighting him. That was all. We started playing yesterday at my house. We'll probably play it at my house tomorrow too." She sat back in her seat and tossed her hands in the air. "I don't know why everyone is making this such a big deal."

Mom leaned even closer to Hank. "You're going back to Maisie's house? For *another* playdate?"

Hank let go of his mouth. "Maisie just said that, didn't she?" Then he pinched his lips once more.

"Of course he's coming back," she said. "Hank is my friend."

His hands fell away from his mouth and he turned so that he could see Maisie. *He was her friend?*

She looked back at him. Her lower lip plopped out and she shrugged.

Hank had had friends when he was in early elementary. He had had two of them, boys who liked dirt and digging and rocks. Together, they would pretend that they were dinosaurs and sometimes rock-eating aliens. But one of the boys had moved away and the other had become interested in baseball and soccer and other things that had nothing to do with dinosaurs, or rock-eating aliens, or Hank. And that had been the end of that. For a while he had tried playing dinosaurs and rock-eating aliens by himself, but it just wasn't the same.

Then, of course, he had discovered his love of rocks as things in and of themselves, and rocks were always fun. Rocks were always interesting. Rocks were always ready to be collected and sorted and polished and held. Rocks never wanted to play something that Hank did not want to play. Rocks never made jokes that made no sense at all. Rocks never sounded annoyed for no reason. Rocks were always just what they were. They were always rocks. Just like Hank was always Hank.

But apparently now he had a new friend. Now he had Maisie—who liked *The Jungle Book* and had a house full of rocks.

"Hank," said the principal.

Hank looked up just for a second, just enough time to feel the prickly *a'a* discomfort of her gaze.

"Hank," the principal said again. "It seems like you have been having quite a few . . . challenges lately. Are you sure everything is all right? Is Maisie telling the truth?"

Hank slid back down in his chair. He pulled his rocks out of his pocket and held them very close to his eyes. He mouthed the word "geode" over and over again.

There was a long pause.

Mom said, "If Hank says he and Maisie were playing, then they were probably just playing. Hank doesn't lie." There was another pause, shorter this time. "That's one of the many great things about Hank."

The principal broke another stretch of silence. "Okay then," she said, pivoting in her chair.

"Okay," said the moms.

"Okay," said Maisie. "But this better not besmirch my personal record."

Hank said nothing, but later, in the newly painted and restored boys' bathroom, he whispered excitedly to his rocks, "I had a fight with Maisie, but now she's my friend and is going to give me a cool rock so shhhhhhhh."

Even friends sometimes bring their moms along for playdates, and Hank's mom and Mrs. Huang thought maybe supervised playdates might be best for a while, "considering . . . ," said Hank's mom.

"You might have a point there," said Mrs. Huang.

"Don't worry," said Maisie, sidling next to Hank and speaking softly. "We won't let them cramp our style."

"What style?" Hank whispered back.

She gave him a big wink. "That's right. We'll leave them guessing."

At Maisie's house they sat in the kitchen and downed the rest of the lemon ricotta cookies. Their moms sat in the living room making the classic mom mistake of thinking no one could hear anything they said.

"She is a piece of work, that Mrs. Vera," they heard Hank's mom say. "That stupid book. It will be the end of Hank."

"Maisie hates it too."

"They all hate it. But Hank . . . poor Hank . . . It gives him nightmares. I begged Mrs. Vera right from the beginning. 'Can't you read something less sad? Can't you let Hank read something else—be somewhere else?'"

"And she wouldn't bend?"

"She never bends. She wouldn't even let him go to the bathroom when they were reading that one book, the one about the girl with the pony. He would weep—*weep*—when he got home. But Mrs. Vera would not relent."

Embarrassed, Hank took a bite of cookie and looked down at his plate.

Maisie stood up. "This is boring. Let's go."

She led him to the garage. "Take your pick," she said, opening the closet full of rocks. "I keep my promises. You can keep what you pick forever, even if you turn out to be a lemon."

"I'm not a lemon," said Hank, sighing as he admired the crowded rows of rocks upon rocks. "Lemons grow on trees."

"Not really a lemon, you goof." Her hair hula-ed sideways. "But a lemon like a bad car, a car that looks good on the outside but is rotten on the inside."

He picked up the apple-size amethyst and cradled it like a baby. "Why would I be rotten on the inside?"

"Exactly. So listen." She lifted her heels off the ground and began to walk in a small circle on her tiptoes. "I . . . am . . . sorry . . . if I was like . . . *Ack! That Maisie is a bulldozer!* I did not mean to break you. Or punch you. Or be mean. Okay?"

He gave her a shy look. "Okay."

"Who I am is just who I am, is the thing," she said.

"Who I am is who I am too," said Hank, his eyes growing wider.

"My mother tells me I need to care a little less sometimes. She says it gets me into trouble."

"My mother tells me *I* need to care less sometimes. She

says it gets *me* into trouble!" said Hank, astounded by the growing number of similarities he had with this girl who was, indeed, a lot like a bulldozer. He pictured a bulldozer with Maisie's face and her swishy black hair. It made him laugh.

She smiled and then laughed too. "Great. Okay. Let's play Jungle Book. For real this time. You're Mowgli but your parents didn't die. We're on the same baby hockey team. That's what we're doing now. Playing jungle hockey. Baloo always plays tricks on you, but you like it." She grabbed two yardsticks from a tub of tools.

Hank shoved the amethyst in his sweatshirt pocket and took one of the sticks.

Maisie led Hank outside. "These are our hockey sticks."

Hank watched Maisie run across the yard.

"Ha ha!" she said. "I actually replaced your hockey stick with an eel, but at first you just think it's a normal hockey stick."

He took a step forward. "Mowgli says this is just a normal hockey stick, and Mowgli isn't worried that his best friend is a bear because bears actually don't want to eat people."

"But then you realize your hockey stick is actually an eel and go all crazy."

Hank looked down at his yardstick. His eyes bulged as he

dropped the stick on the ground and started wiggling and jumping. "Mowgli is going all crazy."

"Don't worry, Mowgli. It's a nice eel. It won't hurt you." She picked up a long twig that had fallen from a tree and handed it to Hank. "Here's your real hockey stick."

Hank had a tingly feeling in his belly, and at first he didn't know what to think of it, but then he remembered. This was delight. This was just like rock-eating aliens back in the day.

"But this turns out to be an eel too," said Hank, dropping the twig and jumping some more. "Mowgli's going all crazy again." He pulled his amethyst out of his pocket. "Mowgli thinks he might also eat a rock."

Maisie started to jump up and down. "Oh, no! That's not a rock. That's a sweet baby hedgehog."

From across the fence Booler started barking. Hank looked up and could see the dog pulling against the end of his rope, staring at Maisie.

"Oh, no, Mowgli, your wolf mom, Raksha, says we have to come home for dinner. Let's go. You can bring the baby hedgehog because it wants to be our friend." Maisie hopped the fence and ran to Booler.

Hank hesitated.

She looked back at him, dropped her chin a fraction. "We're just playing."

She plopped down next to Booler and started scratching his chin. "Raksha says we have to eat bones for dinner. No, Raksha, we want honey."

Booler rolled onto his back and showed Maisie his belly. She started scratching that instead.

Hank hopped the fence. "But Mowgli likes bones so he's happy," said Hank, putting down the amethyst and petting it before plopping one side of a twig in his mouth. "And interestingly, bears also like huckleberries."

Maisie smiled. "Now it's bedtime," she said, dropping on all fours and resting her head next to Booler. The dog wiggled and placed a paw on Maisie's shoulder. "Raksha says you should go to sleep and she'll make you more bones in the morning."

Hank sat next to Maisie. He watched as Booler, his nose vibrating, looked at him. The dog blinked and, in a flash, ran his long tongue across Hank's face.

"He licked me," laughed Hank, even as he turned his face away from Booler's hot, dank-smelling breath.

"That's 'cuz Raksha thinks you're probably not a lemon."

Unexpectedly, Mrs. Vera announced that she had revised the seating chart. Jacob F. needed to switch places with Emma L. Jacob G. needed to switch places with Marcela. And Jacob W. needed to switch with Maisie, which meant that Hank now sat right next to his new friend.

"It's a little suspicious, don't you think?" Maisie asked him after school that day. They were playing tug-of-war with Booler as their moms sat talking in Maisie's kitchen.

When Hank just shrugged, Maisie added, "I mean, putting us together is nice and Mrs. Vera is not normally that nice, is she?"

That observation was certainly hard to deny. And it wasn't just that Mrs. Vera had gotten so mad when Hank burned down the boys' bathroom or that she had gotten so mad when he and Maisie had a fight. Mrs. Vera just generally seemed mad. Well, not really mad, but serious. Part of it was her voice, which did not have all the warm and fuzzy highs and lows of Hank's mom's voice. When Hank's mom was happy, Hank knew she was happy. Her voice got loud and fast and high and every word spilled out of a great big smile. When Hank's mom got mad, he knew she was mad. Her voice got louder and faster and lower and every word spilled out of a great big frown. Mrs. Vera was not like that. Her voice was always the same—no real highs, no real lows, just steady, measured consequences handed out for every little mistake. You did not want to mess with Mrs. Vera.

"She's a piece of work, that Mrs. Vera," Hank said.

"Why does she limp like that?" asked Maisie.

Hank shrugged. "That is a big mystery."

Maisie pulled the tug-of-war toy free from Booler's mouth and threw it just far enough for Booler to reach without tensing the rope around his neck.

"You know what I think?" she said. "I think maybe Mrs. Vera has been replaced by an exact replica—limp and all—from outer space."

Hank stood still. "Do—do you think aliens might replace us?"

"No," said Maisie, grabbing one end of the tug-of-war toy

that Booler had returned to her. "Aliens only replace mean people. It's a well-known fact."

Alien replacement or not, a funny thing happened with the change in seats. Hank began to find the horrible book a little less horrible. To be sure, the book was still heartbreaking. It was also—because of Hank's crime spree—bloated, charred, and smelled like smoke. And every time Mrs. Vera picked it up she would display it to the class like a valuable artifact. Then she would stretch her neck long and say with a holy voice, "You know, the Nazis burned books too. May this be a powerful lesson for all of us."

At this point in the story, the boy was hiding in the forest and living off berries and nuts. He had befriended a stray wiener dog that he named Leah. And Leah was a real hero. An old woman had seen the boy, and she had alerted the Nazi soldiers that a boy like him was in the forest. When a soldier found him, the dog bit the Nazi's ankle, allowing the boy and the wiener dog to run deeper into the dense woods. At first, the forest seemed dark and scary, but then Leah found an abandoned hut for them to live in. And that was all well and good until one day a mysterious explosion sounded and the little dog ran away. Now the boy had been waiting for Leah for two days. And if that wasn't bad enough, it had turned to winter and there were no berries or nuts.

But the new wrinkle in all of it was that Hank didn't cry or feel all *a'a* when listening to the story anymore. Because, now, Maisie sat right next to him. And Maisie spent the whole time drawing pictures of Nazi-fighting dogs.

"That's how you fight *the man*," she whispered to him when she caught him watching her.

He wrote her a note: "Are you saying the alien Mrs. Vera is actually a man?"

Maisie wrote back, "Would that matter?"

Hank thought about it. He printed, "I guess not. She'd still be a piece of work."

Maisie shrugged and started shading her picture.

After that, Hank drew pictures too.

And then there was another surprising development. At recess, he and Maisie started playing Jungle Book. Hank always played Mowgli, but Maisie switched off. Sometimes she played the funny bear, Baloo. Sometimes she played the wise panther, Bagheera. And sometimes she went entirely off script, playing elephants, monkeys—even, once, a very confused and lost kangaroo.

"Me baby! Me baby! I can't find me baby," she said in something that maybe sounded a little like an Australian accent. "Oh, no! Here it is. It's in me pocket. Hiya, man cub, is there anywhere in this bloody jungle where a kangaroo can get a cuppa?"

That one threw Hank for a loop since he knew, of course, that Australian animals like kangaroos would never be found in the Indian jungle. But Maisie didn't mind when Hank raised that very obvious problem.

She just laughed and said, "Ha! Guess I can't fool you. You're right. I'm not a kangaroo. I'm really the evil tiger Shere Khan in disguise!" Her voice grew low and rumbly. "I'm gonna get you, man cub," she said, chasing him across the field.

At night, when Hank's parents would ask about his day, Hank would tell them all about the trouble Mowgli had gotten into.

Mom and Dad would break into big smiles and say things like, "It's nice to have a friend, isn't it?"

And Hank had to agree. "Yes. Friends are even more fun than rocks."

"You should invite Maisie here," said Mom more than once. "Friends take turns. I'm sure Mrs. Huang wouldn't mind."

But Maisie never wanted to go to Hank's house. If they went to Hank's house they wouldn't be able to include Booler, and Maisie said Booler would feel excluded if that happened.

Hank understood. He knew a thing or two about feeling excluded. He knew there were birthday parties he wasn't invited to, valentines he did not receive. It didn't bother him too much. He had his rocks after all. And now he had Maisie. Still, those slights had not been painless, and he would never want Booler to feel the way he had felt on Saint Patrick's Day, when one of the Jacobs offered everyone but Hank a dyed-green snickerdoodle.

Then again, Hank liked his house. He liked the order of it, the predictability of it, the way it often smelled of the cinnamon applesauce that his dad cooked. Hank liked his bedroom and his giant bookcase of rocks and minerals. He wished he could share those things with his friends. That's right: friends—plural. Because he realized Maisie wasn't his only friend. Booler was his friend too.

One day they were scanning Booler's yard for dog poop. Maisie had two plastic produce bags. One was slipped on her hand. The other was held open. Each time she found some poop, she would pick it up with her plastic-bag-covered hand and drop it in the open bag.

Hank was all excited to play Jungle Book because it was always especially fun when Booler got to be Mowgli's wolf mom, Raksha. But this time Cowboy and Honey were in the yard too and, after giving Hank and Maisie a quick sniff and a lick, Cowboy and Honey started sniffing all around the fence, their noses pushed deep into the grass that had replaced all the mud and ice. Maisie's eyes suddenly got very wide and her mouth became a perfect *O*.

"Cowboy and Honey are Nazi soldiers," she said dramatically. "I'm the boy from the book. Booler is my faithful wiener dog, Leah. When the big explosion happened in the book Leah didn't actually run away. She ran to get help and guess what? She found you. You're another wiener dog and your name is . . . Alberto."

She held the bag full of dog poop out in front of her. "We've been collecting all the land mines the Nazis hid. We have a secret way to do it without getting blown up." She froze, a look of alarm on her face.

"Shhh," she whispered. "I think I hear Nazi soldiers."

Hank's body stiffened. It was bad enough he had to listen to that book at school—and now to let it invade his free time? No way. "I don't like that book."

Maisie tiptoed over to Mr. Jorgensen's trash can and threw away the bag of poop as well as the plastic bag she'd used to cover her hand. "Shhh. I better hide these. They can't find out we've moved them."

Suddenly, she dropped to all fours and crawled over to Booler.

Booler tapped his nose against Maisie's nose and went, "Ruroo."

Louder—with real resolve—Hank repeated, "I don't like that book."

Maisie crawled to him. "Shhhh. The Nazis will hear you, Alberto."

Yelling, his jaw pushed forward, he said, "I'm . . . I'm Mowgli!"

Maisie crawled away from Hank and back to Booler, who had gone as far as the rope attached to his collar would take him and was looking intently at Cowboy and Honey, his nose twitching. When Maisie got close, she took Booler's tug-of-war toy and held it up to her face. "Now, if I just adjust this stink bomb . . ."

She fiddled with Booler's toy and then threw it toward Cowboy and Honey, who looked at it briefly and went back to sniffing. "Hurry, Alberto, or the stink bomb will get you. It's gonna be a bad one!"

Hank stared at the dog toy. His hands spun wildly. What was she not understanding? This was their free time! This was the one guaranteed time they did not have to let the sad thoughts of the book in their minds. He would not play this game. There was no way he would play this game.

A gigantic cracking sound broke the silence. Maisie had farted. It was the loudest fart Hank had ever heard. Shocked, he turned to Maisie with big eyes, his hands now limp at his sides.

"I told you it was gonna be bad," she said, laughing. "And it's stinkyyyyyy." She got up and ran to the other side of the tree. Booler followed her, tail wagging at this new mischief. A fraction of a second later the horrible scent of Maisie's fart reached Hank's nostrils.

"It's awful!" said Hank.

"Are the Nazis running away?"

Hank looked over at Cowboy and Honey. Sure enough, they had moseyed a little farther.

"Yes," he said with surprise. Something began to shift and lighten inside him as the sight of the dogs reminded him of the Nazi-fighting dog pictures they now drew at school. "This is how . . . we're fighting the man!" he said, glee brightening his eyes.

"They're going down!" Maisie yelled. "Now we'll finish them off with my other booby traps. Come on."

Hank ran to the other side of the tree. He crouched next to Maisie, who was pulling up handfuls of weeds. Booler pranced in place, eyes on Maisie.

She pointed toward Booler's empty food dish. "First, you bring them the soup in that bowl. Just be like, 'Barkedy bark, I'm a nice dog bringing you soup just to be nice.' Then, while they're eating, I'll sneak up and sprinkle this itching powder on them."

"Ruff," said Hank, running to get the bowl.

"Leah," said Maisie, looking at Booler, "you stay here and guard our hut."

With a quick forward motion she bent down and kissed the top of Booler's head. Then she turned to Hank. "Okay, Alberto. Let's show those stinking Nazis what we can do."

Hank, dragging the food dish, crawled over to Honey and Cowboy. "Barkedy, bark, bark, bark." He dropped the dish in front of the two dogs and sat back on his shins.

"Ruff," he said, tilting his head to one side and letting his tongue dangle from his mouth.

From the other side, Maisie tiptoed over to Cowboy and Honey, whose lazily batting tails suggested that they were willing to play along and at least give the bowl a sniff. Giggling, Maisie sprinkled the loose weeds on the dogs' backs and tiptoed away.

"Oh my gosh, the Nazis are going crazy!" she said, giggling even more now and slapping her thighs. "That itching powder really works."

Hank gave a final "ruff" and then crawled back over to Maisie. "Bark, bark, bark."

"That's right, Alberto," said Maisie. "Look at them tear their clothes off! They itch so much! And now look! They've fallen in the river. And they're naked! And they're floating away!"

She ran back to the very relaxed Cowboy and Honey, her arms outstretched and wobbly. Hank, on his knees, shuffled beside her.

"And don't you dare come back! If you come back you will die! And don't hunt down people who have seizures, because it is evil and you will be cursed forever and ever."

Hank turned, confused. "The boy in the book doesn't have seizures. The boy is Jewish. That's why the Nazis are after him."

She dropped her hands to her sides. Her face was blank, and when she spoke her tone was stiff. "The Nazis killed people who had seizures too. They killed lots of people. Anybody who was different."

Hank let her words sink in. "Did they kill people with autism?"

Maisie nodded. She was quiet for a moment. Then she scrunched her face tight. "But they're not going to get us because we're smarter than them."

She reached down and pulled up another handful of weeds. In a frenzied movement she threw the weeds at Cowboy and Honey. "This looks like itching powder but it's actually a memory potion. Those stupid Nazis won't even remember this forest."

She took a step forward. Chin held high, hands on her

hips, she said, "Don't worry, Alberto. We're the heroes of this story and we're taking those Nazis down."

There was a thud behind them. They turned to see Booler on the ground, his whole body shaking.

"Booler!" yelled Maisie. She ran to him, dropping to the ground and running her hand across his flank. "It's okay, boy. We're here. It's gonna be all right." She sounded like Hank's father when he put on his emergency-room-nurse voice—gentle but certain.

But Hank was not so sure that he believed Maisie. It did not look like the dog would be all right. From his head to his tail, the dog thrashed up and down while his eyes stared blankly ahead and a thread of drool slid out of his mouth. "Is he having a seizure?"

"Uh-huh," said Maisie.

"Can he hear us?" said Hank.

She shook her head. "No. But he wants us here."

Hank sat next to Maisie. "It's okay. It's almost over," he promised as he brushed the top of Booler's forehead with his fingertips. "*Is* it almost over?" he asked Maisie.

"Probably. They don't last too long."

They sat half a minute more, maybe a little longer, until finally the seizure stopped. Booler blinked and looked around. Struggling just a bit, he rolled onto his belly and stood up. He took a few wobbly steps, then a few wobbly sniffs. Then he plopped back down on the ground next to Maisie. He nudged her hand with his nose, and when she started to pet him he rested his head on her knee. With a loud sigh, he closed his eyes and soon began to snore.

They sat with him a while longer, just petting him.

Without much enthusiasm, Maisie said, "Do you want to play the book some more?"

Hank's voice was soft. "No. Booler doesn't like that game."

"No," agreed Maisie. "He really doesn't."

Hank took his three rocks from his pocket. "This is garnet," he said to the sleeping dog. "This is adamite. This is a tiger's-eye."

"Now you see why I wanted you to adopt Booler," Maisie said. She didn't sound like an emergency-room nurse anymore. She seemed liked the saddest, most defeated person he had ever heard. She reminded Hank a little bit of the boy.

She said, "This is too scary for Booler. Imagine what it's like when we're not here."

Hank fumbled with the rocks in his hand. He took a deep sigh. He stood like Maisie had stood earlier—his chin up, his hands on his hips, the total Superman pose. "We're the heroes of this story and those seizures are going down."

Maisie's eyes grew bright. "That's right." She sniffled and her voice grew stronger. "Those seizures are going down and we're gonna save Booler."

Their plan was brilliant and sneaky. Hank went up to his dad on Saturday morning and said the words he had been practicing. "I'm going to the schoolyard to look for rocks."

Dad stood scrambling eggs in a pan. "Don't you want breakfast?"

He rolled back his shoulder, all Clark Kent–like. "I . . . um . . . I'm going to find some rocks. I'm a fan of rocks and also minerals."

His father chuckled. "So I've heard. But I think your mom would want you to have breakfast. Why don't you eat some eggs and when Mom gets back from the grocery store I'll go with you?"

Hank swallowed. He had not expected this inquisition! "So I'm going to find some rocks now. At the school." He rushed out the door and walked quickly, checking twice over his shoulder to make sure his dad wasn't following.

Immediately, he faced a problem. He was supposed to meet Maisie on the field so that he could actually be looking for rocks since it was much easier to tell people you were looking for rocks when you were actually looking for rocks. But the school gate was locked and there was no way he could get beyond it. His hand began to spin again as he bit down on his lip and mumbled, "Rocks, rocks, rocks."

Pebbles. They sparkled up at him from the dirt between the edge of the grass and the school windows. They would have to do. He bent down and started examining the find. They were, without doubt, some of the most unspectacular pebbles he had ever seen. But he examined them. That was the point. To look at rocks and wait.

"Hank!"

He looked up to find Booler and Maisie running toward him. Maisie had attached Booler's collar to a cloth belt. She struggled to keep up with the powerful dog, who pulled and strained left and right with every passing bush or tree.

"Booler is strong!" Maisie yelled. "He's been like this the whole way. When I snuck into Mr. Jorgensen's yard and told him I was there to liberate him, he was like, 'Hallelujah! Get me out of here!'

"He just started running. I said, 'Slow down, boy, you'll

pull my arm out of its socket,' but he was like, 'No way! My life can finally begin!'"

Hank ran toward them, which made Booler even more excited. He pulled so hard that Maisie dropped the lead. The pit bull jumped forward and knocked Hank right down, startling him and sending an uneasy tickle through his body. Then he saw Booler's face close to his, and he smelled the dog's breath and he laughed, even as Booler pinned him down and ran his long tongue all over his face.

"Ew," said Hank. "He licked my teeth!"

"Booler," Maisie said, retrieving the lead. "Get off Hank. You be a good boy."

The dog jumped up. Tail flapping, he shoved his nose in every bush and blade within reach.

"Let's have your belt then," said Maisie.

Hank took off his belt and handed it to Maisie, who unhooked the cloth belt and replaced it with Hank's. Then she handed the makeshift leash to Hank, saying, "You got your story straight?"

"Yes."

"Okay. So when you get home, just tell your story and stick to it."

"I will." He had never felt so determined, so firm.

She saluted him. "Today you save a life."

Hank nodded, the heroism of his deed filling his chest. He started walking home but the dog would not move, and the more Hank pulled, the more the pup resisted. Booler plopped down and stared at Maisie with big brown eyes even when Hank pulled him along the grass.

"Don't do that. You'll hurt him," said Maisie.

"But he won't come. Booler, you gotta come," Hank pleaded. "I'm taking you to your new home. It's a good thing."

Maisie pointed a finger toward Hank's street. "Booler," she said, her voice firm and loud. "Go with Hank."

Impossibly, the dog's eyes got even bigger as he stared at Maisie.

"I think he wants you to come too," said Hank.

Maisie dropped down, sitting back on her heels so she was the same height as Booler. She took both sides of his face in her hands and stared intently into his eyes. "Listen, lovebug," she said, leaning her forehead against the dog's. "If Hank's mom sees me the jig will be up. She's seen us together." She stood back up.

Hank gave the lead another tug. Booler didn't even blink. "You gotta come, Maisie."

Maisie sighed. "Okay. I'll walk most of the way."

But most of the way doesn't amount to much if you can't

get where you're going, and Booler would just drop to the ground every time Maisie tried to slip away. Maisie had to walk them right up to Hank's kitchen door, and only then—only right when Hank had his hand on the doorknob—did Maisie jump into the bushes so that she wouldn't be seen when Hank opened the door and said, "I found a dog," to—it turned out—just Sam.

Sam was sitting in his high chair, the remains of his breakfast spread across the tray. But that was incentive enough for Booler. Booler rushed into the house, put his front legs on the tray, and inhaled every scrap of food left. Then, when he was finished with that, he started right in on Sam's messy face.

That was when Hank's parents returned.

"Sam!" screamed Mom. She lunged forward and pulled Sam out of his high chair. His saliva-covered face reddened as she swung him upside down and every which way checking for missing body parts.

Dad flung himself onto Booler, who—delighted—adopted the new face in front of him as the object of his abundant slobber.

"I found a dog!" yelled Hank, both his hands spinning. "I was looking for rocks. There was a stray dog. It's very nice. I told him he could live here. That is my story and I'm sticking to it."

His mother froze, letting a dazed Sam dangle sideways in front of her.

His father slowly pulled back from Booler, whose tongue got longer as it stretched toward the man's neck.

Mom pointed her finger at Booler. "Wait a minute. I know this dog. This is the dog that lives next to Maisie. You two are always playing with him."

Hank swallowed. He could feel his heart beat. "That's . . . That's a different dog. That's Booler. This is . . . Alberto."

"No," said Mom. "This is the same dog. I recognize it."

Dad's bushy eyebrows almost danced. "Hank. Are you . . . lying?"

There was a pause before Hank said, "That is my story. I'm sticking to it."

Mom widened her stance. She wasn't yelling, but there was a yelling-like sharpness to her. "Hank. Did you take this dog?"

Hank did not stick to his story. The truth tumbled out like towels from a dryer. Hank told them about Booler's seizures and the long rope that kept Booler tethered to a tree. He told them how lonely Booler got, how scared Booler got, how in all his days at Maisie's he had not once seen Booler's owner, how the owner was mean and would not give Booler to Maisie, how Booler was a good dog, a very good dog, and how Booler needed to be rescued, and how only Hank and Maisie could rescue him, how they were the heroes of the story, and how—somehow—the Nazis would actually win if Hank did not adopt Booler.

When he finished telling them everything, his mother nodded. She nodded for a long time and then took a deep breath and blew away the bright sharpness from before. She said, "I hear you, Hank, and I am so proud that you want to help Booler, but now is not a good time to get a dog. Our lives are pretty crazy already. Sam gets into everything the minute I put him down. Soon he'll be walking. I don't think I can manage even one more thing."

"Booler isn't just a dog. He is my friend and he needs to be saved," said Hank.

Dad sat on the kitchen floor and rubbed the dog's tummy as Booler closed his eyes in blissful relaxation. "I'm glad you have a friend like Booler, but Booler belongs to someone else, and that someone must actually be pretty nice to let you spend so much time with his dog. He's probably really worried about where this guy has gone."

Maisie burst through the kitchen door. "He's not missing Booler! All he does is feed him. He doesn't deserve such a good dog. He thinks Booler should be tied to a tree because he has seizures, but—"

"But different isn't less. That's what you're always telling me," Hank interrupted.

His parents both took deep breaths. They looked at each other, and by the time they let out long sighs it was as if they had had a whole conversation.

Dad shook his head. "You can't just save someone's dog." He didn't sound angry, but he didn't sound all that sympathetic either. He picked up the improvised leash and stood. "Let's go, Maisie. I'm taking you and Booler home."

"No!" Maisie yelled. "You have to save Booler." She fell on her knees and planted herself next to the dog, who sat up and nudged her with his nose. With a flick of his tongue he dabbed her cheek.

Hank plopped down beside her. He threw his arms around Booler's neck. This wasn't right. They were supposed to be the heroes of the story and here his parents were messing everything up.

Maisie craned her neck to look up at Hank's parents, her eyes darting back and forth between them. Maisie did not look like she was going to cry, but there was something going on on Maisie's face, something that made Hank uneasy. Whatever it was, it had turned her cheeks and chin a splotchy red and made her eyes wide and . . . maybe "wild" was the word. He kept one hand on Booler's shoulder and moved the other onto Maisie's.

Her voice was pinched and rushed, as if she did not want to speak but could not help herself. "You have to save Booler," she repeated. "That's the plan. Get Hank to want Booler and then get Hank to save Booler. That was always the plan."

Mom's face became the one that was unreadable. To the same degree that Maisie's face had grown red, Hank's mom's face became chalky. Like Maisie's, her eyes were wide, but her mouth kept getting bigger and rounder. When she spoke, Hank understood. She was mad. She was crazy mad.

She growled, "Excuse me?"

Maisie seemed to shrink. The splotches on her face grew redder.

"Maisie, did you *use* Hank to help you take this dog?"

Hank looked from his mom to Maisie, who, for once, had nothing to say.

"It's time to go home, Maisie," said Dad, who was now using his own angry voice, which was never as scary as Hank's mom's but could still freeze puddles. He pulled suddenly on the belt attached to the dog's collar. Booler stood, expectant.

"Let's go," Hank's father repeated.

But Maisie did not move.

Booler, his eyes on Maisie, stood solid, his muscles distinct and stiff.

Then Maisie was up, walking out the door, Dad and the now tail-wagging dog trailing behind her.

Mom put Sam back in his high chair. She turned in a circle and then let out a long breath. She began to pace the length of the kitchen, her eyes scanning the floor, her fingertips pressing her temples.

This was a mom Hank had never seen. Her shuttered mouth, her downcast eyes, her heavy, fast feet. It made him uneasy. But he also knew what he knew—what his mom always said, what he always trusted her to believe. "Different is not less. That's what you say. Just because Booler is different—"

His mother stopped, looked at him hard, and for the first time he could remember with her, he had to look down. The *a'a* feeling began to stir.

"You should go to your room, Hank. Go to your room."

What had he done? He did not understand what he had done to provoke . . . this—this non-mom, this scary, *a'a*-sparking non-mom who, clearly, did not believe that different was not less, who did not believe that Booler deserved a good home, who did not appreciate all the work he and Maisie had gone through, who did not do what she was supposed to do, what he always needed to count on her to do. Not yell. Not stare. Not make him feel bad. Keep the *a'a* at bay. That was her job. That was her promise. That's what he needed.

Hank began to tremble. He wanted to flee, spin, storm, cry, and crawl into a little ball all at the same time. Instead, he ran to his room and slammed the door. His screams coiled round his eardrums, making him cover his own ears with his hands.

Sloppy tears streamed from his eyes and he felt the world gnash at him with its sights, sounds, smells, and surfaces. His belly and head felt heavy and sluggish while his limbs demanded to move like the Flash and, unsure how to process all those things, he threw himself on his bed and yelled, "Booler!"

Finally, when his screams turned into hiccups, Mom came to him, his little brother resting on her hip. From the lightness of her step, the soft blankness of her expression, he knew the non-mom had gone. The mom he counted on was back.

She put Sam on the floor and sat on Hank's bed. She ran her fingers down his hot, wet scalp. "You're really sad, huh?" But her voice did not have the highs and lows he expected.

She sounded almost as flat as Mrs. Vera. She sounded tired.

"I know you really wish you could keep Booler. It's hard when we can't get what we want."

The disappointment of it all washed over him again and his lungs shivered when he took a deep breath. "Booler really wants to live here."

She started to rub his back. "You are sweet to want to help this dog. But I'm sure Booler is happy where he is. Dogs don't like change, just like you don't like change."

"But Booler's owner is so mean to tie him up like that."

"I'm sure his owner thinks he is doing the right thing and I'm sure he loves Booler. He probably doesn't want Booler to get hurt."

"But I really want Booler."

She was silent for a minute. Then she repeated, "It is really hard not to get what you want."

His lungs didn't shiver anymore when he breathed. Instead, he just felt really tired and a little sore.

"You want a hot dog?"

He shook his head.

"Are you sure? They usually help you . . . even things out."

He sniffed and, eyes shut tight, whispered, "Okay."

She cleared his bed and handed Hank's least favorite

stuffed bear to Sam, who began to drool on its ear. Then she bent forward and helped Hank shift his body sideways and slide down to the end of his mattress.

"You ready?"

He gave a little nod and she started to roll him—just like a jelly roll—inside his down comforter.

Hank had been doing "hot dogs" for as long as he could remember. One of his doctors said they might help combat the *a'a*. And they did. But they always left him craving real hot dogs too—the broiled ones, not boiled. The boiled ones were disgusting.

Once the comforter was wrapped around him like a heavy, safe cocoon, his mom stood back and said, "Here's a nice hot dog in a nice bun. What do you want on your hot dog, Hank? You want ketchup?"

The comforter nodded.

"Here comes the ketchup," she said, squeezing his feet with her hands and then working the tight squeezes all the way up to the top of his shoulders. Hank felt his body loosen and relax.

"You want some mustard?"

"Yes."

She worked the squeezes up, again, from his feet to his shoulders. "And onions?"

"Uh-huh."

By the time she was done he had about everything a person could think of on his *hot dog*, including french fries, Tater Tots, chicken soup, potato chips, and even ice cream.

"You feel better?" she asked, her voice now returning to its normal peaks and valleys.

"Yes," he said, and, indeed, between the weight of the comforter and pressure of the squeezes, everything had evened out in his body, the prickly outside, the heavy inside. It all felt, well, like just one thing. Like just Hank.

He sat up, ran his sleeve across his runny nose, and, sighing, said, "Will you broil me a hot dog?"

His mom tilted her head and said, "Hmm. Now why did I think you might ask that?" She picked up Sam and held her hand out to Hank.

He took it and they walked into the kitchen.

Hank's parents told him that they needed to talk. Hank figured this was coming. When it came to his parents, whispering always led to talking, and his parents had been whispering, whispering, whispering every since his dad returned from Maisie's. Now—a full day after the spoiled Booler rescue—the time for talking had come.

Hank, Mom, and Dad were sitting cross-legged on the floor of Hank's room while Sam napped. Hank was fingering his three rocks of the day (fluorite, biotite, and phengite) in his right hand even though Mom had placed a bowl of marshmallows in front of him. Usually they only had marshmallows when they went camping. So what was the deal with these marshmallows? They seemed wrong. And he didn't want wrong marshmallows, just like he didn't want wrong talking—talking where all he got to do was listen to a list of the things he had done wrong. It would make him feel bad—worse, embarrassed—and he didn't want to feel bad or embarrassed. He had just gotten over feeling bad about the whole Booler thing and embarrassed about his whole mountain-of-a-meltdown thing.

He thought maybe they would bring up Booler but they didn't. They brought up Maisie, and when they said her name they said it with a funny bite in their voices. No. Hank could tell that this was not going to be good at all. So he kept his head down, his eyes on his rocks. He put them down on the carpet and started to move them around like little cars.

With soothing voices, his parents said they wanted him to think about whether Maisie had been a good friend.

He told them, "Yes. She is my best friend."

But that did not seem to convince them. Like they were reading him a picture book about bunnies and lambs, they started asking him questions, one after another, oh so gently.

How did he know Maisie was a good friend?

Did she take turns?

Did she ever let him choose the game?

Did she ever want to come to his house?

Did she really care about Hank or did she only care about Booler? Had she actually wanted to be Hank's friend or had she really wanted to use Hank to get what she wanted?

Hank didn't know what to say. Hadn't they wanted him to have a friend? Hadn't they been so excited to hear about the games he and Maisie played? Did they not want him to be friends with Maisie now? Is that what they wanted? Because that was not what he wanted. He liked Maisie. Maisie was more fun than rocks.

"We just want you to think it through," said Dad.

"We just don't want people to take advantage of you," said Mom.

There were things Hank knew for certain—things he never doubted because he never needed to doubt them. There were three kinds of rocks. Different wasn't less. Sam had a bottomless supply of drool. Those were indisputable facts—and so was Maisie's friendship. Wasn't it?

He shook his head. "Maisie is my friend." But somewhere in the back of his mind a caterpillar of doubt yawned and stretched and began to get ready for work. Because wasn't it also a fact that his parents were right about so many things—especially when it came to people? Weren't they right about Mrs. Vera being a piece of work? Weren't they right about the neighbor boys who didn't play with him being too loud for him anyway? When his one remaining friend who loved rock-eating aliens moved on to other interests, hadn't his parents been right when they told him that real friends don't make you change for them, real friends accept you for who you are? So were they right this time? Was that possible? Were they right about Maisie?

"You're wrong," Hank declared, his voice certain, even as the caterpillar of doubt finished its breakfast and put on its chrysalis and began its slow, steady metamorphosis into the black moth of revenge.

When he woke up the next morning he wouldn't talk to his parents. They had awoken the caterpillar—they had made him doubt not only Maisie but also his ability to know when someone was really being a friend to him. Now, his parents would pay. He wouldn't talk to Sam, who loved the people who had awoken the caterpillar and would thus also pay. He wouldn't talk to Maisie, who maybe, possibly, his parents had been right about, who maybe had been using him, who maybe hadn't been his friend after all. And he had really liked having a friend too. She would pay the most.

There was only one problem. She refused to pay! When she sat down next to him at school she started yakking away, spoiling his revenge by not even realizing it was happening.

"So the good news is your dad did not talk to Mr. Jorgensen," she said as the other kids in class found their seats. "I thought for sure he would because he had that whole spill-the-beans look going on the entire time he was walking me and Booler back. Luckily, he only spilled the beans to my parents—boy, were they mad. They told me I had to march right over to Mr. Jorgensen's house with Booler and apologize, but I told them that George Washington never apologized for freeing our country so I didn't see why I should apologize for freeing Booler."

Hank imagined himself a stone wall.

"Unfortunately, my parents do not seem to appreciate Mr. George Washington, which I think is un-American of them."

Hank did not respond. Luckily, Mrs. Vera called the class to attention.

At lunch, Maisie was at it again, starting right where she left off, willfully ignoring how well Hank was icing her out.

But Hank persevered: When she sat down at their usual lunch table, he plopped down at another. She got up and moved next to him. "They still made me go over and apologize to the old liver spot. But I was tricky. My parents watched from our yard but they could not hear me, so when Mr. Jorgensen opened the door, I was all, 'I am so sorry, Mr. Jorgensen. I rudely took Booler for a walk without asking permission and that was terribly wrong of me and I will never do it again.' Pretty smart, huh?" Maisie nudged Hank conspiratorially with her shoulder.

But he just crossed his arms, squinted, and made his mouth an angry wrinkle.

Maisie continued. "So now I have to clean the whole garage by myself because apparently I make bad choices and that's supposed to help me."

When he still didn't answer, she added, sounding less sure of herself, "But I'm thinking maybe I'll be able to bring you some rocks from our rock cupboard." She moved to the other side of the table, where Hank had been pointedly looking. She moved her head left and right so that he could not help but see her smile. "Yeah? Some rocks?"

But Hank would not be soothed, not even by rocks, and he kept his distance even when the bell rang and it was time to head home—when they normally planned a playdate or talked about homework or compared notes about what a piece of work Mrs. Vera was.

At home, the freeze-out continued. But it was harder because when his parents figured out he wasn't talking to them, they just went about their usual business as if it didn't matter at all.

Finally, he had to put on his jaw-clenching angry face and say, "You gave me a bad day. I didn't have any doubts that Maisie was my friend until you said something."

His parents were in the kitchen cooking dinner. They

looked at each other. His mother bent down and hugged him—but he knew how to punish her. He did not hug back at all.

"We're sorry," said Dad, coming to rest a hand on Hank's shoulder.

"She fooled us too," said Mom sadly. "I really thought she was made of better stuff than that."

Hank's heart seemed to give a little squeeze. So it was true then. Their sympathy seemed to prove everything. Maisie had been using him all along.

He ate his dinner without tasting it and didn't even feel better when they sat down and watched *The Jungle Book*.

Funny enough, though, Maisie still kept acting like nothing had changed between them. The next day, while waiting for Mrs. Vera to come walk them to class, she said, "The thing is, I don't see how cleaning the stupid garage is supposed to help me make better choices, especially when I already make good choices. So I think my parents are just Cinderella-ing me, which seems like it should be against the law. What do you think?"

Hank looked at Maisie. He pushed out his jaw and billowed his lower lip, just like he'd seen his mom do, and he glowered at her. He could tell he was doing it really well too, because he could feel his eyebrows trembling. It must have worked because Maisie didn't try to connect with him again until lunch, when she pushed a brownie across the table toward him. She seemed humble and small, but Hank just pushed the brownie away and went to look for rocks. It should have been fun. It had always been fun before. It had always been enough before. But something had changed. It was like someone had taken all the spice out of his guacamole and left him with just smashed avocados. He missed the spice. He missed Maisie.

When the school day ended he followed her outside. He ran up to her and said, "Real friends don't try to use you."

Her shoulders slumped forward and she began to rake her hair in front of her face. In a singsongy mumble, she said, "It is maybe a little bit true that when I first met you I was being nice partially so you would take Booler." She blinked and her curtain of hair fluttered. Her voice stronger, she added, "But then I beat you up by accident and now we play Jungle Book and stuff. And . . ." She threw her hands in the air and they fell down with a defeated flail. "And I thought you wanted to save Booler too. I thought that's what you said."

"I did want to save Booler too. But my parents said . . . They said maybe you only cared about Booler, that maybe you weren't really my friend."

She pushed her hair out of her face and looked at Hank,

astonished. "We *are* friends." Quietly, she added, "You're my best friend."

Hank leaned back. His face softened. "Really?"

"Of course, you goof." She gave his arm a gentle slap.

He smiled. And the black moth of revenge fluttered away.

She smiled back and, taking a step forward, said, "Now let's look for rocks—but good ones. Maybe we can find a meteorite. We could give it to a museum and make them name it after us. We could call it the Huang-Hudson meteorite."

Hank held his hand up to stop her. "Meteorites are named after the place they're found."

"Then we're keeping the meteorite for ourselves."

"No," he said as his confidence began to blossom. "It is a fact that friends don't fool each other, but it is also a fact that they don't boss each other around. And if we find a meteorite we have to give it to a museum because that is what you do."

She looked at him, nodded approvingly. "Okay, Mr. I'm-not-a-doormat. I like it! We'll give it to the museum."

She took another step forward. He stopped her again. "And it is also a fact that friends don't make you change for them. Friends accept you just the way you are. And friends don't ask you to give them your toys or your money or your food. And they don't just play at their house. They also come to your house"—with that one he gave her a pointed look—"and—"

"And when they fight they make up! I get it! Let's find that meteorite!"

They walked toward the playground.

She pulled her mouth up to one side and said casually, "I'm still a little insulted that you thought I was using you, Hank. I'm not a lemon, you know."

"No," he agreed. "You can't be best friends with a lemon."

At dinner he said the same thing. His parents were talking about the tooth that had that morning popped out of Sam's gums. They couldn't get over it. Mom was showing Dad pictures of the tooth on her phone even though both of them could have just looked over at Sam in the high chair and seen the real tooth for themselves.

Hank blurted, "You can't be best friends with a lemon."

His parents looked blankly at each other, then at Hank.

Mom put her phone on the table. "Excuse me?"

"You can't be friends with a lemon. Maisie isn't a lemon so she wasn't using me. You were wrong. And friends have fights and then they make up. So . . . I think you need to make up with me."

Dad scooped some more applesauce onto Hank's plate. And they made up.

Hank was in Paradise. Literally. With him and Maisie having made up, Maisie's family had invited him to see the Lewis Overthrust that weekend, a mountain pass where Maisie's dad had been working with a team of geologists to better understand the places where earthquake faults come to an end. Her parents had explained to Hank how the pass's bent and contorted bands of light-colored quartzite had—over millions of years of intense compression—pushed themselves on top of younger, darker rocks until the landscape looked like folds of ribbon candy.

Afterward, they had parked at Two Medicine Lake and hiked up to Paradise Point for a picnic. It was fully spring now. The meadows were carpets of green and the leaves in the trees danced in the light breeze. In the distance they could see Flinsch Peak, which Maisie said looked like a giant gray traffic cone. It sort of bothered Hank because he didn't think anyone should describe something as impressive as a nine-thousand-foot matterhorn as if it were as ordinary as a traffic cone, but Hank was in too good a mood to make it a big deal. He did know an interesting fact about matterhorns, though, and decided to share that instead.

"That is actually a matterhorn," he explained. He had just swallowed a bite of one of the many ham and cheese sandwiches he had brought to share, and he was still holding the sandwich up to his face. "An interesting fact is that a matterhorn is carved out by at least three glaciers. Three!"

He waited for Maisie to answer, and when she didn't he turned to her. She was staring right at the steep peak. He repeated, "A matterhorn is carved out by at least three glaciers. It takes millions of years." She continued to stare. Hank waved his sandwich in front of her face, trying to catch her attention. "Maisie?"

Mrs. Huang slid closer to her daughter and put her arm around her as Mr. Huang got up. He was thin and tall with short, spiky hair, and when he stood he looked a little like a long green onion. He said, "You really know your stuff, Hank. Hey, why don't we start heading back down the path and I can tell you about the time I climbed to the top of Mount Thielsen in Oregon?"

"I'm not so interested in climbing mountains," said Hank. "I just like facts about mountains. And also rocks."

Mr. Huang chuckled. "Well, then you'll like this. Mount Thielsen is not just a mountain. It's a dead volcano."

Hank waited for his voice to catch up with his percolating brain. He whispered, "This is the best day of my life," stuffing the remainder of his sandwich into his backpack. He shouldered his pack and started to follow Mr. Huang back down the path, adding, "Do you know that a dead volcano has a volcano skeleton?"

"I do," answered Mr. Huang.

They talked all the way back to the car, and it was only when they got there that Hank realized Maisie and Mrs. Huang were not behind them. "Hey, where's Maisie?" asked Hank.

Mr. Huang looked back up the path. "Oh, they'll probably be here in a minute. Maybe they saw some good rocks!"

"Yeah. Though I don't know how I could have missed any," said Hank.

When Maisie and her mom did arrive, they all got straight into the car. Maisie seemed pretty quiet. But then, it would have been hard for her to get a word in edgewise since Hank had so many things he wanted to say about what they'd seen, and—best of all—Mr. and Mrs. Huang did too. And so Hank didn't even mind when he looked over and noticed that Maisie had fallen asleep. He just kept talking, and when he looked at the time and noticed that they had been driving for over an hour, he said, "Do you have to drive this far every day?"

"Most days," said Mr. Huang. "But it won't be forever."

"You should camp up here," said Hank. "I saw campsites near Paradise Point. That would be easier and more fun."

"We used to camp a lot." Mr. Huang's eyes flashed in the rearview mirror. "Remember when we used to camp, Maisie?"

Hank looked over. Maisie was awake. Her brows were knit tight. She snorted, "No."

"We camp all the time," said Hank. "You guys can come with us sometime, but you'll have to bring your own sleeping bags because Sam is going to use the extra one from now on."

She snorted again and said, "Not bloody likely."

Hank tilted his head, not sure if she was talking about the camping or the sleeping bag.

"What Maisie is *trying* to say," said Mrs. Huang calmly, "is that we don't camp anymore. And now we don't need to because we are always so close to the wonders of nature. It's in our backyard!"

Mr. Huang turned on the radio and music started playing. "Hey, it's your favorite song, Maisie!"

Maisie let out an exaggerated sigh. "Not this version. Only old people like this version."

Hank listened. It was not a song he knew—and he didn't think he liked it. It was a warbling man singing, "Oh, we can beat them forever and ever. Then we can be heroes just for one day."

"No way," said her dad. "Nothing ever beats the original!"

Maisie sat up straighter. "You don't know what you're talking about!"

Hank was confused. Something had changed. The tension of only a moment ago had seemed to dissolve. But that couldn't be right because the words Maisie and her dad were saying were actually arguing words. He looked cautiously up at Mrs. Huang, who was doing something on her phone.

Mrs. Huang said, "Okay, okay, how about this?" and a different version of the song began to play.

"That's better," said Maisie.

"Oh, no!" cried Mr. Huang.

Maisie laughed. So Hank laughed too, and he listened. When the song ended, he said, "That is a much better version of the song, Mr. Huang. Maisie is right."

Maisie looked over at Hank. Grinning, she said, "Yeah, Dad. You don't know anything."

"Not about music," said Hank, before diplomatically adding, "but you do know a lot about rocks."

They took the turnoff for Meadowlark and soon Hank was delivered to his parents with a sunburned face and a container of oatmeal cookies.

Hank held the cookies in front of his dad. He said, "Maisie made these for us. I told you she wasn't a lemon."

"You were right," said Dad, grabbing a cookie from the container and taking a bite. "And we were wrong."

Hank rolled his eyes. "You *were* wrong."

Mom came. She took a cookie too. "She's a tornado, that one, but I think her heart is in the right place."

Hank took his own cookie and lorded his wisdom over them again. "Her heart *is* in the right place. Otherwise I think she would die." Then, humming the song from the car, he went to his room and slipped a rock he'd found at Paradise Point on his bookshelf.

Hank was still thinking about his day trip with Maisie's family the next time she came over to play. They had invented a game where they organized Hank's rocks and minerals by their likelihood of becoming money in the aftermath of a robot uprising. There was a lot to consider: beauty, weight, potential for being used as a robot part.

They were debating the possible value of a piece of coral-colored quartzite. Maisie was convinced that the plain-looking rock would have absolutely no monetary value, but Hank disagreed.

"People could throw it at the robots."

"Yeah, but people aren't going to pay for *throwing* rocks. They'll be able to find those anywhere."

"Yeah, but it would be a really good throwing rock. People would want it. It's super hard. It's the exact same stuff as in the Lewis Overthrust. It got so compressed that it turned from quartz to quartzite. That's a valuable anti-robot weapon. It would really dent them right up."

She rolled her shoulders and looked away. "Ugh. I don't want to talk about the Lewis Overthrust."

"Why?" said Hank, who could think of nothing more exciting to talk about than the day of their picnic.

She deflated a bit. "I just . . . Let's get back to organizing."

So they did, and it was great, but to be honest even Hank realized that it wasn't as great as playing at Maisie's. For one thing, Maisie's house came with Maisie's parents, who would occasionally toss him an exciting rock fact. For another thing, there was Booler. Booler was Hank's friend too, after all. And Hank increasingly shared Maisie's worries about excluding Booler. Booler did get so excited to see them. He would bark and jump as soon as they appeared, and when they reached him he would burrow into them and let out high-pitched little whines as his tail flippity-flopped left and right.

Plus, Hank saw now that Booler really did need them. For example, the dog had developed a small sore on one of his paws. It did not look too bad to Hank, just a little redness between two of his toe pads, but Booler licked it constantly. Maisie said that her old dog used to do the same thing and that it was not a good sign. She started bringing a jar of Vaseline with her over to Mr. Jorgensen's, and she and Hank would take turns gently spreading a thin layer of the greasy cream on the sore. The Vaseline would settle Booler down for a while, but only a little while, so then they would have to look at him and say, "No, boy. No licking." That worked too, until Booler figured things out and started waiting for them to play before he started licking his paw, which meant that, now, one of them had to keep an eye on him the whole time they were visiting him.

It worked. In less than a week Booler was better, but the whole event raised an important question. What would have happened to Booler's paw if they had not been there? And if the sweet pup needed so much attention to help him recover from a sore paw, how much more did he need to keep him safe during his seizures?

"I think Booler really needs to live with me," Hank told Maisie one day.

"Duh," she said, letting her tongue fly outside her mouth. "Of course he should live with you."

"Too bad my parents don't want a dog."

Maisie was quiet for a minute. She got a sneaky look on her face. "Or maybe your parents just *think* they don't want a dog."

And so the lobbying began.

To the argument that Hank's mom didn't believe she could "manage one more thing," Hank and Maisie explained that Booler would not mean more work for anyone. Booler would mean less work for everyone because Booler would keep away burglars and play with Sam, who had just one day earlier taken his first steps—right in front of Maisie and Hank. Sam, they said to all who would listen, would appreciate a four-legged nanny as fun as Booler. Plus, Hank and Maisie could even train Booler to do things for Hank's mom, like open cabinets and drawers and bark if Sam were about to walk off a cliff.

To the argument that you couldn't just take other people's dogs, they explained that Booler was so lonely and scared and that, surely, a creature's right to feel safe and loved was way more important than a neighbor's right to keep an animal he didn't even appreciate.

To the briefly mentioned and quickly withdrawn argument that a special-needs dog would be too much trouble, Hank said, "I have special needs. Am I too much trouble?"

"It's like they're a bunch of bully goats," said Maisie.

"You mean billy goats."

"No, bully goats. They get all mad and say nay, nay, nay." She bit into an apple and rested the side of her head in her palm.

"Isn't it horses who neigh?" Hank asked.

Maisie paused her chewing. "Irrelevant."

Finally, they decided to take legal action.

"To whom it may concern and also Mr. and Mrs. Hudson," said the carefully printed letter that Hank and Maisie deposited in the Hudson mailbox. "We hold these truths to be self-evident, that people and dogs are created equal and that they are both born with the inalienable rights of life, liberty, and the pursuit of happiness. And even if a dog belongs to someone else, if that someone else denies a dog its inalienable rights, then that dog can choose a new family. Amen. God bless America."

In return they received their own letter. They found it in Hank's lunch box the next day.

It said, "To whom it may concern and also Hank and Maisie: Even if we wanted to, there is nothing we can do, inalienable rights notwithstanding. Let the record show,

Booler is tied to a fifteen-foot-long rope and has lots of room to move around. Booler has a doghouse for shelter. Witnesses, including one Mrs. Huang, mother to Miss Maisie Huang, note that Booler's owner brings him inside when it's really cold. Said owner also feeds and visits with Booler numerous times during the day and does far more than just feed Booler. Said owner provides frequent attention, love and—importantly—anti-seizure medicine. In addition, Booler has two dog friends—known henceforth as Cowboy and Honey—who also provide Booler with daily visits and love. Until such time as legal authorities prove otherwise, we rest our case. In other words, Booler stays put."

Hank shook his head. "It's like they can find a logical answer for everything."

"They have an answer, all right," said Maisie, suddenly excited. "An answer to all our problems! Your mom's letter gave me a great idea. They want legal authorities; we'll give them legal authorities. You don't have a phone, do you?"

Hank shook his head.

Maisie's lips plopped forward as she let out an annoyed blast of air. "My parents are cheapskates too. Come with me."

They walked toward the school office.

"Where are we going?" asked Hank.

"You'll see," said Maisie.

"But it's almost time for class."

"It'll be okay."

"But . . . there are birthday cupcakes today. One of the Jacobs brought them."

"Don't worry. Ain't nothing getting between us and birthday cupcakes."

They entered the office, where the woman who guarded the principal's office sat at a desk, a big pair of earphones covering her ears. She moved the earphones down to her neck and smiled.

Maisie smiled back and said, "Um, can I use the phone? I have to call my mom."

The woman readjusted her glasses. "Now, Maisie, you know the phone is for school business."

"This is school business."

"And what school business is that?"

"I think I forgot to take my medicine today."

The woman's chin wobbled as she tutted, "Oh, my. You just leave that to me."

"No. I can do it. My mom wants me to be more independent about these things."

The woman considered this before saying, "Well, okay. You can call from there." She pointed to a telephone at an empty desk and then, picking up a file on her desk, walked over to the supply room next door. "Let me know if you need any help," she hollered, as the steady *thrum thrum* of the copy machine filled the air.

Maisie walked over to the phone. She glanced at the supply room and then picked up the phone and dialed. There was a pause, and then Maisie said, "Hello, Mother . . . um . . . did I forget to take my medicine this morning?"

Through the receiver Hank made out Mrs. Huang's barely audible voice.

"That's good. I couldn't remember. Thanks."

She hung up the phone and then picked it up again. She looked from side to side and then gave her lips a confident smack.

Hank watched her fingers press the buttons 9-1-1 and he looked down at the desktop when she said in a low, throaty whisper, "Hello. This is an anonymous tip. There is a man being verrrry mean to his dog. He lives at 1306 Frankel Street. Good day—I said good day!"

Quick as a flash Maisie hung up the phone, grabbed Hank's wrist, and pulled him all the way, running, to the end of the schoolyard, where they collapsed on a bench and each gulped a mouthful of air.

Hank dropped his hands onto his thighs. He wasn't sure if he was excited or proud or about to walk off a cliff. So he just sat there, stunned.

Maisie flung her head back. Her hand rose and fell on her heaving chest. "That was a close one," she said. Once their breathing had slowed back to normal, Maisie continued, "So you're probably wondering why I take medicine."

"No," said Hank, who was still trying to figure out if he should panic or crow or just get ready for the promised birthday cupcakes.

"Really?" Her head darted up with a surprised look on her face. Then her head darted back down. "Well, good. Because that is personal business."

About forty-five minutes later two police officers entered the classroom. They were dressed mostly in black—black jackets, black pants, black shoes, black hats. But they had blue shirts, the collars of which peeked out from their coats, and they had yellow badges that shone justice for all—including dogs. The woman police officer had a dark ponytail. The male police officer had glasses and a red nose that he wiped from time to time with a mysteriously never-ending supply of fresh tissues. They stood next to the principal, and when Mrs. Vera saw them she frowned before shuffling slow as ever over to them. Hank watched the grown-ups talk and then he glanced over at Maisie, who was staring at the police officers with a smug smile on her face.

Mrs. Vera spun around. Her face was purple—and she was glaring at Hank and Maisie. Suddenly, it was very clear to Hank which emotion he was supposed to feel. It wasn't excitement. It wasn't pride. It had nothing to do with birthday cupcakes. He had walked off the cliff and was belly flopping straight onto the asphalt.

Mrs. Vera stood over their desks and boomed, "Maisie and Hank, I don't know what you were thinking, but you go with these police officers right now."

Hank looked at Maisie, and when Maisie stood up and followed the police officers down the hall he did the same, even though his whole body felt *a'a* and his hands were spinning like crazy.

And when Maisie shouted over her shoulder, "We were saving a life! A life, gosh darn it!" Hank face-palmed—they were doomed.

Here was a surprise. Apparently, reports of animal abuse were supposed to go to animal control—not 9-1-1, which was for life-and-death emergencies. And callers were not supposed to make accusations and hang up without giving their names. Calling 9-1-1 for inappropriate reasons—from a school phone—could get a person suspended or even expelled.

"I don't even know what you are talking about already. I only phoned my mom," Maisie replied when the facts were laid out in this way. "You can call and ask her."

"The call came from the phone you used, Maisie. It was

about your next-door neighbor. And you just admitted to an entire classroom that you were 'saving a life,'" said the principal.

Hank could barely breathe. The jig was really up this time. He snuck a peek at Maisie. She was taking short breaths through her open mouth. Her gaze kept shifting left and right. It seemed to Hank that even Maisie was doubting her ability to get them out of this one.

But then Maisie stood up, looked right at the principal, and said, "I did not call 9-1-1, madam. How dare you accuse me in this way? Lots of kids at this school live near me. Any one of them could have called. They see how that old man keeps his dog tied up to a tree—everyone does. Now good day!"

Hank watched in awe as she stormed out of the room, her head leading her feet.

The principal shook her head before turning her attention to Hank. "Now, Hank," she said, her voice softening. "No one thinks you did anything wrong. Just tell the truth. What happened?"

The urge to spill the beans pushed at Hank like a wave, but he stood his ground. He stood up and—eyes on the carpet—repeated Maisie's words. "I did not call 9-1-1, madam. How dare you accuse me in this way? Now good day." And then he ran to the bathroom and hid in one of the stalls until Mrs. Vera came and found him.

"That's quite a caper you two pulled," she said, holding open the stall door, her voice as unreadable as ever.

He looked down at his shoes, not sure what to say.

Her shoulders fell forward and she sighed. She held out her hand, a peace offering. He took it and they made their way back to class.

"We're just trying to save Booler," Hank explained, filling the silence in the empty hallway.

"Booler?"

"He's a dog. He's like the boy in the horrible book, only seizures are after him, not Nazis."

"Is that right?" Mrs. Vera was quiet for a long time. When they were near the classroom she squeezed his hand a little tighter. "I guess I could keep that secret."

He looked up, surprised. Sensing opportunity, he added, "So . . . um . . . is it time for the cupcakes?"

"Just about," she said before letting out another loud sigh. "But I'm afraid that—good cause or not—people who lie about calling 9-1-1 don't get birthday treats, not in my classroom."

Hank turned his head just enough to see Mrs. Vera's face. She was looking straight ahead, that funny little half smile of hers pulling at her mouth. He really did not know how to make sense of her at all. One moment she was yelling at him, the next she seemed all understanding and nice, and then right after that she was practically pulling cupcakes out of his mouth. He would ask Maisie her opinion. He really did not think Mrs. Vera was an alien, but he knew that his mom was right. She was a piece of work, that Mrs. Vera, a real piece of work.

"Hank had a big day today," his mother said to his father at dinner. She spoke with a mysterious sort of energy that reminded Hank of a vibrating phone. It was terrifying.

They were sitting at the table. Well, all of them were sitting at the table except Sam. Sam had finished eating and was toddling around the kitchen. This was the way it was with Sam now. He was always toddling. It was like the minute he learned to walk he decided he wanted to run. So he would take two steps, speed up, and fall right over. Then there would be a tense moment when Hank would wait—his breath held tight in his throat—to see if Sam would start to wail. Hank hated when Sam cried. For one thing, the volume hurt his ears. For another thing, it was just so annoying. It was a high-pitched worm that crawled through his brain.

"Is that right?" Dad asked. "Tell me about it, Hank."

Hank's mom rested her hand on his dad. Her eyes grew large and Hank knew that this was it. He would be in trouble for sure. He moved the food around on his plate, saying nothing.

Mom plowed ahead. "Hank," she said in a voice that almost seemed like a laugh. "Lied. Again."

The table became still. Dad put down his fork and looked at Mom. "What?"

Hank stabbed a roasted potato wedge and shoved it into his mouth.

"Hank lied again." Mom explained the phone call she'd gotten from the principal about the 9-1-1 incident. She ended by saying, "Everyone knows it was Hank and Maisie, but I guess they can't prove it so they're dropping the whole thing and hoping the two of them have learned their lesson. The point is, Hank lied. Our Hank. He *lied*. The time with Booler wasn't a fluke. He is lying regularly now."

Dad's head turned slowly from Mom to Hank. Hank shoved another potato wedge into his mouth and chewed as fast as he could.

"Buddy," said Dad. "Good job!"

Hank almost choked. Everybody always said that lying was a bad thing. They always said that one gift of autism was that it made him especially honest, and now here he was getting congratulated for lying like a common lying liar.

Dad kept talking. "I mean, no, it's not okay to lie to your principal or—especially—the police. You can go to jail—I mean, you're not going to jail. Don't worry."

Dad put a hand on Hank's shoulder as Hank froze in place, his eyes and cheeks bulging.

"What I'm trying to say," said Dad, "is that lying is a big step forward for you. Some kids on the spectrum never master lying! It's a milestone. We're super proud of you."

But it turned out that milestones were a little like birthday cupcakes. They sometimes came with strings attached. And the strings wrapped around this particular milestone involved a joint punishment for both Hank and Maisie. It was horrible! Their parents had conspired together on it. Each of them was grounded for a week, was stuck with extra chores, and had to apologize in person to the man himself, the cruel Mr. Jorgensen.

Maisie was outraged. "It's a complete injustice," she insisted when they talked about it at school the next day. "My parents are always complaining about people who don't care about anything but themselves, and here I am caring about something that isn't me and they make me do yard work, a lot of yard work. I have to weed the garden, and plant tomato seeds, and—get this—I have to turn dirt over. That's right. I have to shovel up dirt and mix it like a salad. My parents say it's a real thing, but I think they're just making stuff up."

It wasn't the chores that worried Hank. It was the apology. He hated apologies. People were always expecting to be looked in the eye during an apology—even his mom expected it—and that always left him feeling so hunted, and he just knew that Mr. Jorgensen would be the type to not only give him the old eyeball but to expect the old eyeball in return. And as the day wore on and the time for the apology grew nearer, Hank began to feel like he had a bowling ball lolling about in his belly.

The plan was for Maisie and Hank to walk to Mr. Jorgensen's straight after school. But—what with that bowling ball in his stomach—Hank found himself shuffling more than walking.

Maisie started to get irritated. "Hurry it up. I want to get this over with."

Hank peered at her and shuffled even slower. "You are doing that thing where you tell me what to do."

She screwed up her face like she was about to yell something. Then she sighed and began to shuffle beside him. "Fine."

They arrived at Maisie's house to find Mrs. Huang waiting

for them on the front porch. It had been a long time since they had needed Hank's mom at their playdates, but she had promised to be there, just in case Hank needed a little pep talk before meeting the old man. But she wasn't there, and Mrs. Huang explained that she would not be there until later because Sam had run into a tree and wouldn't stop crying. And that meant that Hank would have to apologize without getting a pep talk.

He tried to stall. "Can I have some water?" he asked.

"Yeah. I need some water too," said Maisie. She dropped her backpack on the porch and snuck a glance at Mr. Jorgensen's house. "And maybe a snack?"

Mrs. Huang pulled her mouth into a little ball. "Fine," she snapped. "But only vegetables."

They went into the kitchen, where she gave them water and dropped a plate of carrots and celery in front of them. Hank ate slowly, eager to drag things out, and he knew that Maisie was trying to do the same thing because he saw her slump over and then, a minute later, pretend to be asleep.

Mrs. Huang sighed. She said, "Hank, why don't you wait outside for a little while? I think Maisie needs a little mom time."

Hank had not been hungry anyway. He went and stood on the porch and peered down the street for his mom.

He heard barking and turned to see Booler straining at the end of his rope, begging him to come and play. Hank twisted back and forth on the porch column closest to Maisie's door. He peeked again at the dog. He had never been to Mr. Jorgensen's without Maisie and he definitely did not want to do so today. But Booler kept barking, and his mom kept not coming, and Maisie kept having mom time, and so finally Hank mumbled, "Okay, boy. I'm coming."

He hopped the fence and sat next to the dog. It was weird visiting Booler without Maisie. Make no mistake, Booler delighted in seeing Hank. When Hank scratched Booler's belly, one of Booler's legs did a shaky happy dance all by itself. But the visit was also quieter. After a while Hank took his rocks out of his pocket.

"This is hematite. I got this from the rocks and minerals store in Bozeman," he said, holding a shiny steel-colored stone in front of the dog's snout. "And this is marble. I also got this from the rocks and minerals store in Bozeman. And this is just a rock. I found it camping with my mom and dad. We like to camp."

Booler looked from the rock in Hank's hand up to Hank's face. Then he blinked and nudged the boy's head with his nose.

"Which rock is your favorite?" Hank asked. "I like the hematite. It's very smooth. Wanna feel?" He pulled the rock across a flank of soft, silver fur. Booler dropped his head onto the ground and closed his eyes. A small smile spread across Hank's face.

"Well, hello there." A man had snuck right up on them.

Uneasiness tickled Hank's throat, which suddenly felt dry. Surely, this was the evil Mr. Jorgensen himself. The man looked evil enough. He had a wrinkly neck and a suspicious amount of big brown spots on his loose and crepe-papery skin. His hair was thin and almost colorless. It was like an invisible beige, like a blend-into-a-person's-beige-face kind of beige. If that wasn't bad enough, he stood behind a very aggressive-looking walker. It wasn't like the aluminum ones Hank had sometimes seen pushed by patients in the hospital where his dad worked. No. This seemed more like a scary, off-road-vehicle sort of walker. It had a bright red metal frame with thick black tires that could cover uneven ground. Plus, confusing the very purpose of a walker, it had a little basketlike thing in the front that attached to a little seatlike thing in the back. It was almost like the walker could not decide what it was supposed to be, and the sheer indecision of the walker paired with the well-documented cruelty of the man worried Hank.

When Hank didn't say anything, the man said, "Cat got your tongue?"

Hank swallowed in the hopes of finding some moisture

in his mouth. "My tongue is right here," he said, sticking his tongue straight out while he spoke.

Mr. Jorgensen chuckled. "Oh, that's a good thing." He took one hand to pull up his too-loose pants, then he swiveled the walker around and sat on the little seat-thing.

"How you doing, Booler?" said the man.

Booler moved over to the man and bumped him with his nose. The dog let his tail flop from side to side as the man cupped his snout and wiped the sleep out of his eyes.

Honey and Cowboy came running forward. They ran straight toward Hank, and when a quick sniff convinced them that it really was Hank and not his robot clone, they sprang toward Booler.

Now excited, the three dogs retreated to the tree and began to sniff one another's behinds.

The man stuck out his arm. "Frank Jorgensen."

Hank looked at Maisie's house—willing her, his mom, someone, to come—as he gave the liver-spotted hand a quick clap.

"You the friend of Maisie who helped her call the police?" Frank asked. "My goodness, that almost gave me a heart attack."

Hank finally looked up at the man. "Is that why you have that walker? In case you have a heart attack? Because I don't think that will help."

Cowboy came and bumped against the walker. Frank reached down and scratched the dog's head. "No," he answered in a way that made him seem not entirely evil. "The walker is because I have low vision and a bad hip."

Confused by this glimpse of humanness, Hank shifted in his seat. He thought carefully about his next words. "What is low vision?"

Frank scratched his forehead. "In my case it means that things look kind of flat, like on a piece of paper, not in 3-D. And even then I can't see too many of the details."

Hank held up two fingers. "Can you see how many fingers I'm holding up?"

Frank pulled a thick magnifying glass out of the basket and brought it up to his face. "Two."

Hank crossed his eyes and said, "Can you see the face I'm making?" A moment later he pulled back from the giant crossed eyes staring out from the man's magnifying glass. Hank said, "It seems like you see all right."

Frank shrugged. He put the magnifying glass back in the basket. "You're gonna have to trust me."

Hank uncrossed his legs and sat on his calves. "Okay."

Frank's shoulders rose up and dropped. He cleared his throat. "You get old, things happen. It's not always pretty."

Hank nodded. "Yeah. My dad had to have a mole removed from his back once."

"Oh, well, I certainly hope that worked out."

Honey knocked into Cowboy, and Frank began to take turns scratching their heads.

Booler came and sat next to Hank, who tried to copy Frank's head-scratching technique. He looked again at Maisie's house, and when he still did not see her, he spilled out the words he had practiced with his mom. Sounding a little rehearsed, he said, "I am very sorry that we called 9-1-1 about your dog. We should never have done that." He paused and then added, "And I'm sorry you almost had a heart attack."

Maisie's neighbor nodded. He scratched his nose and then cleared his throat again. "I appreciate you saying that. I really do. And I appreciate your concern about Booler. It's a tough situation, that's for sure. But, you know, I love Booler. I rescued him. I found him in a box near the side of the road when he was just about a month old. Somebody just dumped him there. The poor thing was thin as paper."

Hank imagined a puppy made of lined paper—a puppy both real and somehow unreal—all alone in a box near the side of the road. It had Booler's big eyes. He could hear it whimper.

"Was he starving?" Hank said, remembering the starving boy in the book, the one who had now left his little hut to go find Leah and food.

"Oh, he could barely keep any food down, he was so starved. But I nursed him back to health." The man paused. He stood and wheeled his walker closer to Booler, who sat right up, eager for the man's attention. Frank leaned over and petted the pit bull's head before adding, "You hurt me really bad when you accused me of neglecting poor Booler. I don't like leaving him out here, but his anti-seizure medicine doesn't work perfectly, and in the house there are too many things Booler can crash into if he has a seizure. He's had to get stitches three times already because of that. And it's really a bear getting Booler to the vet too. Truth is"—he lowered his voice to a whisper—"I'm really not supposed to drive anymore."

Hank squirmed, confused. Frank Jorgensen did not seem that bad. Then again, the man's coldheartedness was undeniable. Hank dropped his head so that his chin grazed his chest. "I'm sorry," he muttered.

"And I appreciate that, like I said," said Frank.

"No," said Hank, lifting his head just enough so that he could see the man's neck. "I mean . . . I am sorry . . . but you did not fix Booler's sore paw. Maisie fixed it."

Frank sat again on his little seat. He frowned. "No," he said doubtfully. "I don't think—"

Hank lifted his head a little more. "She did. She—we—put Vaseline on it every day. And Maisie picks up all the dog poop in your yard."

The old man leaned back in his seat. Hank watched him scan the grass and then scratch his chin.

Finally, Frank said, "Dog poop doesn't bother dogs, so that is not really necessary, but . . ."

"I'm sorry we called 9-1-1, but . . . Maisie says maybe Booler should live somewhere else."

From the corner of his eye, Hank watched Frank look over at Maisie's house. Then he looked back at Hank, who dropped his gaze.

"Here's the thing," said Frank, rubbing his palms back and forth on the legs of his pants. "Booler would have the same problem anywhere he lived. It's sad, but this is what is best for him. This rope and the open space of the yard are the only things keeping him safe. Besides, he has Honey and Cowboy. They're great company."

Honey and Cowboy *were* great company for Booler. Hank could see that. As excited as Booler got when he saw Hank and Maisie coming over to play, nothing got Booler's tail swishing more than the chance to sniff Honey's and Cowboy's butts.

"We are Booler's family," said Frank. "Would you like to be removed from your family?"

Hank looked up to see his mom and Sam listening at the fence. Maisie stood nearby.

His mom hollered an introduction to Maisie's neighbor, and then a few minutes later, Hank exchanged a sheepish glance with Maisie as he left her to make her own apology. And as he walked home he thought about what Maisie's neighbor had asked. He knew he would not want to be separated from his own family. His family was his greatest weapon against the *a'a*. They were his fire-resistant volcanologist suit. They were his heavy-soled boots. He would not quit them for anything. But what did that mean for Booler? Was there really nothing they could do for him? Was he really destined to spend the rest of his life tied to a tree?

He asked Maisie what she thought. They whispered as they did their math in class the next day.

"Don't listen to Mr. Jorgensen," insisted Maisie. "Honey and Cowboy get to come and go as they please. They have a doggy door. They're all, 'La-de-da, we get to go wherever we want because we don't have seizures. We get to play chase. We get to sniff bushes. We get to sleep inside and have sleepovers with friends who give us sugary doughnuts for breakfast. We get to have all the fun in the world and never worry about anything and our lives are better than yours.'"

"I'm pretty sure Mr. Jorgensen doesn't give Cowboy and Honey doughnuts."

"Urrg," said Maisie. "The point is that Booler gets less. It's not fair that he gets less. He deserves what everyone else gets."

"Yes," said Hank, thinking of all the things Frank had said. "But Mr. Jorgensen gets less too. He doesn't get to have Booler in his house. He's not supposed to drive his car."

"He shouldn't drive his car. I've seen him. Man, that's a scary thing."

"The point is, Booler is part of his family. He wants to be with him. He just can't be with him all the time. That doesn't mean he shouldn't get to see him ever. Would you like to never see your family again?" He said it like it was the most reasonable question in the world, like it was plain common sense.

Maisie's mouth fell open. Agog, she said, "What? Are you taking Mr. Jorgensen's side now?"

"I'm taking Booler's side," said Hank firmly. "Family counts."

Mrs. Vera's head spun toward them. "This is math time,

not talking time. Are you talking about math, Hank? Are you talking about fractions? Multiplying fractions?"

Hank dropped his head. Shook it. He could feel the eyes of the class on him, but he didn't care. Family did count. He knew it did.

Maisie nudged him and handed him a note. It read, "Fine. But clearly further investigation is in order."

8.

"I'm a master at investigating," said Maisie. It was two days later. They were in her garage—and they were not even looking at rocks. They were plotting to figure out if the mysterious Frank Jorgensen really thought of Booler as family or if he was just saying that so people would leave him alone and let him mistreat Booler all he wanted.

Maisie had drawn a blueprint of Frank's property on a big piece of paper. It included the fence separating their yards, the backyard, the maple tree, Booler's doghouse, Booler, the toolshed near the back fence, and a big square representing the house itself. Along the big square she had drawn short, darker lines that stood in for the windows.

With the tip of a pencil she pointed at the fence. "We begin here," she said with such conviction that Hank knew that she must be right. "We very sneakily hop the fence like we always do." She moved the pencil tip to the drawing of Booler. "Then we're all, 'Hi, Booler. We're just here to see you like we always are.' Then, one of us distracts Booler—because remember, he is a very good watchdog—while the other quietly peeks through the windows and looks for evidence."

Hank nodded. "What kind of evidence?"

Maisie pulled her hair into a ponytail and held it like that for a minute. "We'll know it when we see it."

That being the case, Hank told Maisie she could be the one to look through the windows, because he was quite sure that he would not recognize good evidence when he saw it.

The plan started out perfectly. They snuck out of the garage. They hopped the fence into Frank's yard. Hank distracted Booler by showing him his rocks of the day (garnet, pyroxene, graphite), and Maisie ran back and forth from the windows to collect evidence, which was harder than it looked because the windows were dirty and, of course, one of the windows was actually covered in wood. Still, she persevered.

"Okay," she whispered as she ran from the first window back to Hank. "There is a really tiny laundry room where he keeps all his dog supplies—including dog biscuits. Have you ever seen him give Booler a dog biscuit?"

Hank shook his head. Already they were finding such good evidence! "I've never seen him give Booler any food."

She pointed a finger at him and looked like she was about to say something. Then she dropped her hand and said, "Actually, he does feed him breakfast and dinner. I've seen that."

She ran back to the house and peered in a second window. She rushed back, her expression furious. "Get this! Get this!" she said in a hoarse whisper. "Cowboy and Honey are sleeping on Mr. Jorgensen's bed! On. His. Bed!"

Before Hank could answer she ran back to look in another window, but this time she just turned around and ran back. "Abort mission! Abort mission! He's coming. He's coming." Flustered, she plopped next to Hank. She tossed her hair back and smiled. "Just act casual. Pretend we're talking—no, pretend we're singing!" She started swaying and singing the song they had heard in the car. "Though nothing, nothing will keep us together. We could beat them, forever and ever." She nodded at Hank, trying to get him to sing along. "Oh, we could be—"

"Heroes," sang Hank nervously as he remembered the words. "Just for one day."

"I thought maybe you had a question for me," said Frank. He was breathing kind of hard and did not seem nearly as friendly as before.

"A question?" said Maisie, shaking her head and looking

at Hank. "I . . . um . . . no . . . no question. Do you have a question, Hank?"

Hank swallowed.

Frank pinched his lips together and leaned forward on his walker as he looked at Maisie. "It's just that I thought I saw you looking in my window."

Maisie licked her lips. She whispered to Hank, "I thought you said he couldn't see."

Frank tilted his head. "I can see a big blurry head through a window. And I can hear perfectly."

Maisie swallowed and began to pull on the bottom of her shirt.

"Um," said Hank, thinking fast. "Do you have any cool rocks?"

This seemed to surprise Maisie's neighbor. "Rocks?"

Maisie's eyes widened. "Hank is obsessed with rocks, Mr. Jorgensen. That's why I was looking in your window. To see if you had any."

Hank was pretty sure Frank would see this for the lie it was, because at first the man sighed and frowned. But then Mr. Jorgensen scratched his stubbly chin and said matter-of-factly, "I might have a few fossils. Found them in the central part of the state probably—I don't know—forty years ago. Why don't you come see?"

He led them to the small house. Then, leaving his walker at the back door, he guided them past rooms stuffed with furniture and boxes. Although Hank was not about to say anything to Maisie about it, he could see why Mr. Jorgensen didn't want Booler in there. One seizure and Booler would collapse into a pointy end table, or a pointy bedpost, or a pointy file cabinet. It was a real danger zone. In fact, it was treacherous for anyone moving about in that house—Mr. Jorgensen included.

Cowboy and Honey fell in behind Hank and nudged the backs of his knees. "You have a lot of stuff," said Hank, glancing at the dogs, who looked up at him and sniffed.

Frank chuckled. "You sound like my daughter, Colleen. She is always telling me to clear some of this stuff out." He led them into a tiny bedroom. "But, see, you never know when things might come in handy." He reached for a box from a shelf inside the closet. When he began to wobble a bit, Maisie put a hand on his arm.

She said, "You want me to get that?"

He pulled his arm free. "I can do it." More kindly, he said, "Thank you."

He took the box and placed it on a bed covered in a ratty pink quilt. Dust particles floated into the air and began to dance around as he shuffled the contents of the box, finally pulling out two pieces of tan-colored sandstone, each about the size of a jam-jar lid. Dark, feathery lines crossed each rock. He held them close to his eyes and then handed one each to Maisie and Hank.

Maisie looked closely at hers. "What kind of fossil is it?"

"It's from a pine tree," said Hank.

"That's right," said Frank, impressed. "Probably a redwood." He nodded at the fossils. "You can have those." He still sounded more businesslike than friendly, but Hank was never one to look a gift rock in the mouth.

It was a complicating factor, that gift. Because what did it mean? *Was there an ulterior motive?* was the question. Was it a bribe—a means of shutting them up, keeping them off the scent of Mr. Jorgensen's cruel and neglectful nature?

Hank didn't think so. He was really starting to like Mr. Jorgensen.

But Maisie was more skeptical than ever. "I've played this game a million times," she told Hank. "You can never get something for nothing. If you could, I'd have figured out how."

They were in Hank's kitchen eating pretzels. They had wanted to put some space between themselves and Mr. Jorgensen so that they could sift through all their evidence without attracting suspicion. From the doorway they could see Hank's mom in the living room. She was on her hands and knees attaching a slippery sort of padding to the edges of the coffee table. She called it babyproofing. She was doing it everywhere. Apparently, it was supposed to keep Sam from cracking his head open if he fell, just like all the annoying locks she'd put on the cupboards were supposed to keep Sam from eating something he wasn't supposed to eat.

It was all a little *a'a*, frankly. Hank's home, once so comfortable and predictable, was suddenly so . . . well . . . different. It was a weird kind of different too, a different that no one else noticed, no one else wanted to notice, a different that—if you pointed it out to anyone—they would just get mad and say, "It's just padding. Don't you want your baby brother to be safe?"

"He's definitely a tricky one, that Mr. Jorgensen," said Maisie, taking a pretzel and trying to nibble off the salt. "You know what I think? I think we can't just investigate. I think we need to go undercover."

"Hello, sir," said Maisie when Frank, accompanied by Honey and Cowboy, answered the door. She reached her hand past the dogs and held it out to her neighbor, who gave it a limp shake. He did not have his aggressive walker, and, like before, he kept one hand propped on the door frame.

She said, "My associate and I are interested in performing good deeds for absolutely no other reason than because we are do-gooder sorts of people. Might you, perhaps, have some odd jobs you would like us to do for you?"

From the corner of his eye Hank watched Frank pull himself taller and give his head a little roll.

The man sighed and said, "Look, Maisie, I wasn't going to say anything because I know you have your reasons, but now this has gone beyond Booler. You seem to think I cannot take care of my own property. Peeking in my windows . . . picking up my dog poop. I am as capable as I've ever been."

A nervous shiver ran through Hank. Frank had not been yelling, but everything about his words and his tone stank of yelling.

But Maisie barely seemed to notice. Calm as could be, she said, "I don't know what you're talking about, Mr. Jorgensen. We just want to do good deeds. You see, we are do-gooder sorts of people. When people see us walking down the street, they are all, 'My goodness, there go Maisie and her associate, Hank. They are always making the world a better place.' It's sort of our brand."

Frank started to close the door. "Well, that's very nice, but—"

She took a step forward. "Actually, it's for school."

The man squinted. "School?"

"We have to help a neighbor and then write about it."

Hank moved to the side of the porch, the better to distance himself from Maisie. A school project? To help a neighbor? That was definitely not part of the plan. The plan was to go undercover, pretend to be do-gooders, figure out whether Frank was really nice or mean—figure out what was really best for Booler. Hank licked his lips and looked over at Booler, who was asleep in the grass. He twisted the belt loop of his jeans.

The door squeaked open a little. Frank said, "For how long?"

Hank turned around and saw Maisie shrug, so, holding his breath, he stepped even farther away and did the same.

Maisie's neighbor was quiet for a while. Sounding reluctant, he said, "Well, my dogs are always itching for walks. How would that suit you?"

"We would be delighted, sir. Wouldn't we, my-associate-Hank?"

His voice flat, Hank said, "We would be very delighted, sir."

"You watch, Hank," said Maisie as the three dogs pulled them through the neighborhood. "If we keep this up, we'll be so knit into Mr. Jorgensen's life that he'll be telling us where the bodies are buried."

Hank stopped. "There are buried bodies?"

She gave his shoulder a lazy slap. "Figure of speech. He'll be showing us his true colors, what he's really up to—you know, about Booler."

They walked on some more. "Look how much Booler likes his freedom," said Maisie. She sounded so content, so happy, even as she suddenly lurched forward, her arm pulled taut as Booler pounced at a butterfly that had landed on a bush.

It was true. Booler had never seemed happier. His whole face was stretched into what no one could deny looked like an actual smile, and he had a spring in his step as he gave up on catching the butterfly and pranced through the bush.

"But look how much he likes to be with Cowboy and Honey," said Hank, as the dog went and squeezed between Honey and Cowboy, knocking his head against each of theirs.

Clearly, the undercover business would take a while.

So they kept it up. And every day they went to Frank Jorgensen's house, he found them something to do. And every time they did something, he seemed to relax a little more and become friendlier. They walked the dogs. They bathed the dogs. They walked up to the pet store and picked out a new cushion for Booler's doghouse.

"You know, we can do other things besides help with your dogs," said Maisie when they came back with the cushion.

"My, my. This school project is really taking a long time," said Frank. "Well, let me see if there are any non-dog-related odd jobs I can come up with."

The next time they came by he handed them the newspaper. "Maybe you can read me the sports page," he said.

So they did.

It turned out the man was crazy about sports—all kinds of sports, especially bowling. Before retiring he'd even owned a bowling alley.

"It was right on the main street of town," he told them. "They turned it into a Dairy Queen."

"Wait," said Maisie. "There used to be a Dairy Queen here?"

There did, but it had gone the way of the bowling alley, as had many businesses that used to be in Meadowlark. There was no longer an Owl Pharmacy. There was no longer a Coast to Coast Hardware. There was no longer a Moonlight Café or a Hank's Bikes—that's right: Hank's. Over the years they'd all been replaced with cute little souvenir stores or cute little dress shops that catered to the day-trippers going up and down the mountain. Frank told them all about it.

Hank loved listening to Frank's stories. They were like excavations—not for precious metals or jewels, but for the past. And Hank thought it was cool that just like you had to move a lot of dirt to find a diamond, you also had to sweep away a lot of the present to find a forgotten gem. Like a bike store named Hank's. Like a bowling alley that had just six lanes and made all its money on beer (which Mr. Jorgensen told them to keep secret; he didn't want their parents to think he was corrupting their young minds).

Hank didn't keep it secret—not even for a day. He told his parents all about it. His mom even remembered the bowling alley. She'd gone there as a kid. And she'd worked at the Dairy Queen when she was in high school!

"Here's a funny story," Frank said one day after Hank and Maisie read him an article about a woman who had just broken a bowling record. "Booler is what Colleen used to call the bowling alley. When I would come home from work she'd say, 'How was the Booler, Daddy?' I'd almost forgotten about it until I found Booler." He cupped the dog's face in his hands. "When he was a pup, he made this face. It looked just like one Colleen made when she was a baby—but don't tell her that because she will not appreciate the comparison. But the expression . . . It just made me think, 'Booler.' That's how he got his name." He moved around on the seat of his walker. His eyes sparkled.

Maisie thought that was the best story she'd ever heard. She wrapped her arms around Booler's neck. "Isn't that a funny story, Booler? You're named after a bowling alley."

Booler yawned and licked her nose.

But the school project/do-gooder plot was starting to bother Hank. The more time he spent with Maisie's neighbor, the more he knew he was right. Frank was not a two-faced sneakypants. He was a nice guy, and not just that. He was a little like Booler. He wasn't tied to a tree, but Hank wondered if maybe he kind of needed to be. Not really, of course, but maybe sort of, in a way.

The thing was, Frank was kind of a hazard to himself. One time, he was in the kitchen making them ham and cheese sandwiches. He was cutting a tomato because he had this crazy idea that tomato belonged on the same sandwiches as ham and cheese. The man almost cut his finger off. The big knife came *this* close. Hank shuddered. Maisie too. And Frank went right on slicing the tomato, not noticing a thing. And there was evidence that sometimes Frank wasn't so lucky. He was always walking around with Band-Aids all over him. But the tomato incident was the last straw. After that, Maisie took the big knife and threw it in the outside trash. She didn't say a word. She just did it, and Hank was glad.

And then there was the time he answered the door with a big red mark on his arm.

"What did you do?" Hank asked.

"It's nothing. Just a little burn. Can barely feel it," said Mr. Jorgensen.

"But how did you get it?"

Frank got a little snippy then. "I said it's nothing. So that means it's nothing."

But that didn't stop Hank from bringing Mr. Jorgensen some special cream the next day. "My dad said to give this to you," he explained. "He says it's good for burns."

"I can take care of myself," Frank answered grumpily. But he took the cream and held his magnifying glass up close to it so he could see it better. Then he softened. "I mean, thank you."

He didn't want any do-gooding that day. He said his hip was hurting and he just wanted to rest, so Maisie and Hank went out back to play Jungle Book with Booler. They were feeling a little disappointed, actually, because they had been looking forward to some interesting do-gooding. And then things just got worse because Booler had another seizure— and it was a long one, at least a full minute.

They stayed with him, reassured him, petted him—just like always—but after it was over Booler was especially tired. He crawled into a little ball and began to snore before he even closed his eyes and fell asleep.

Maisie seemed even quieter than she usually was after witnessing one of Booler's seizures. Finally, she said, "So Mr. Jorgensen loves his dogs, and his dogs love him and each other. Right?"

"Right," said Hank, who was fiddling with his rocks of the day (all quartz—white, pink, and pale green) and still trying to shake off the drama of the long seizure.

"And, actually, Mr. Jorgensen is not a bad guy."

"He's a good guy."

Maisie nodded. "Yeah. He's a good guy. So Booler probably *should* keep living with him."

This was the first time Hank had ever heard Maisie say anything like this. He turned his head, looked at her. He couldn't read her voice. He couldn't read her face. He waited for her to say more.

Maisie twisted sideways. "But if Booler lives with his family he will always be tied to a tree."

"Mr. Jorgensen says it's the only way." Hank shook his head at the misery of it all.

"And that's because he can sometimes barely take care

of himself." She stood up, frustrated. She began to pace. She stopped, chewed for a moment on her thumbnail. Sounding like she was working out a math problem, she added, "If Booler stays with Mr. Jorgensen he will be sad because he'll always be tied to a tree and alone most of the time. But if he lives somewhere else he'll be sad because he won't be with his family." She looked at Hank. "Does that mean Booler will always be sad?"

Hank came and stood next to her. As close as he was to Maisie, even *her* gaze could be scary, so he turned and looked at the dog. "He doesn't seem sad now."

Maisie looked at Booler. She chewed again on her thumbnail and then wagged her finger at Hank. "No. But does it mean he'll never be one-hundred-percent happy?"

That was a tough one. Hank crossed his arms and thought.

She shook her head. "It's just like the book. If the boy stays in the forest he'll die because there's no food. But if the boy goes back to his village he'll die because the Nazis will get him."

Hank's jaw dropped. "It's nothing like the book." He scowled. "And don't talk about that book. I hate that book."

"But it's not fair," she said, her arms swinging up and then falling in a huff. "It just seems like there should be some way that Booler can win, but . . . what if there isn't?"

Hank went and sat back down next to Booler. He ran his hand across the dog's side. "It's not a contest," he said softly.

She let out a loud "Pffff. That's what people say when they're already winners."

Hank's class was about three-quarters of the way through the gigantic and distressing tome. It was clear to everyone that a merciful book would have ended by now, but as Mrs. Vera liked to say, "It was a long, merciless war. Don't fool yourself by thinking otherwise."

They had been assigned to make a shoebox diorama that showcased the use of metaphor in the book. Hank and Maisie had been assigned the line, "Winter assaulted the little hut, sending missiles of ice and bullets of sleet through the broken windows." Maisie had already made a little cabin out of Popsicle sticks and now she was trying to fill the inside of it with white beads, which was the closest she could come to sleet.

Hank had committed to a silent protest. Well, it wasn't

really silent. He was humming Maisie's favorite song, which was now his favorite song. This was something they did now, when the conversations between them came to a lull. They hummed or sang their favorite song, and when they got to the "Oh, we could be heroes" part, they would bob their heads and shoulders and yell the refrain. Of course, he could not yell the refrain in class. That would draw attention to his silent protest, his nonparticipation in the diorama, which only Maisie was allowed to know about.

Maisie respected his protest, even though it meant she had to do all the work herself. As she said, "I am an expert at dioramas."

Hank had actually not seen Maisie for two days. She had simply not shown up for class. When he asked her where she'd been, she said, "Blah. I had to go visit my doctor in Missoula."

"I like the doctor," said Hank, happy to be reminded of a very interesting talent he possessed. "I have a trick so that it doesn't hurt when you get a shot. The key is to—"

"Don't ask why I was at the doctor either," said Maisie, "because that is personal business, sir. I will thank you not to bring it up."

He didn't bring it up. He asked her instead if she wanted to go camping with his family. They were going that weekend.

She shook her head. "Not happening," she said. "My parents are opposed to camping."

"But your dad said he liked to camp. Remember? He said you used to go all the time."

"Well, we don't now. And I don't want to talk about it." She was quiet for a moment more. Then she looked up suddenly and blurted, "Guess what? Mr. Jorgensen drove his car into a ditch. The police had to drive him home yesterday."

Hank pinched his face in shock and distress.

Maisie reached out her hand and gave his shoulder a squeeze. "He's okay, though. My mom went and checked."

They decided they should go visit after school and both were surprised when a woman opened the door. She was thin with pale cheeks and ponytailed beige hair. She wore a long-sleeved, collared shirt that she tucked into tan pants, and in her hands she held a fluffy white dog the size of a loaf of bread. It wore a thin pink sweater, and matching pink ribbons were tied to its pancakelike ears. Hank might have thought the dog stuffed were it not for the quivering nose that pointed back and forth from Maisie to Hank.

Maisie squealed in delight. She stretched out a hand to pet the dog. "That is the cutest dog in the world."

The woman took a step back and turned to shield the dog

from Maisie's fingers. In turn, Maisie froze, her hand still hanging in the air. She looked at Hank. She looked at the woman, whose mouth was now a squiggly line. Then she looked back at Hank. Something about Maisie's rolling eyes and open mouth worried him.

"Who are you?" said Hank, taking control of the situation.

The woman's head snapped back. "Colleen Jorgensen. I'm Frank's daughter."

The dog let out a series of high-pitched yaps that seemed to mimic the sharp, no-nonsense tone of the woman's introduction.

"I bet I know who you are," said Colleen with a grumble. "You're the kids who accused my dad of neglecting his dog. He loves that dog, you know."

Hank felt a flutter in his stomach. He leaned toward Maisie and decided to let her take control of the situation instead. "Is she mad at us?"

Maisie tilted her head thoughtfully. "I . . . We know he loves Booler. So do we."

The woman moved her mouth from one side of her face to the other and considered them. The dog stretched out its head and began to sniff them from afar. The woman blinked. The dog blinked.

"Do you need something?" said Colleen, who definitely did not seem like she wanted them to need anything.

Hank looked out at the lawn. "We just came for a visit."

She shook her head. "Maybe later. We're pretty busy right now." Then, with something halfway between a weak smile and a hiccup, the woman closed the door right in their faces.

They stood there for a moment, unable to move.

Maisie opened her arms wide. "What the heck?"

"I don't like her," said Hank, frowning.

Booler started to howl and they went to comfort him, but they had not been with him two minutes when Colleen opened the back door. Still holding the little dog, she snapped, "Excuse me? Did anyone say you could be back here?"

"Colleen," they heard Frank say.

She turned her head toward the house and listened to words they could not make out. "Well, I don't think either of us need that distraction right now. We have a lot to work out." She snapped her fingers and pointed toward the fence. "Go," she mouthed at them. "Go!"

They went, but not before privately nicknaming Colleen "the evil daughter."

Details of her visit leaked out the next week, courtesy of Maisie's mom, who Maisie said was the original master of investigating.

"*Apparently*, the evil daughter lives in Minnesota. She's here for a week and she never puts her prissy little yapper dog down on the ground," Maisie told Hank at school on Monday.

On Tuesday she told him, "*Apparently*, the evil daughter is a lawyer, and she was sort of a big deal smarty-pants when she went to high school, but she has always been tough as nails so we really don't want to mess with her."

On Wednesday she said, "*Apparently*, Mr. Jorgensen fought in a war a long time ago, but not the one with Nazis. And then he opened his bowling alley and the evil daughter actually went to college on a bowling scholarship even though she hated bowling and called it stupid. And Mr. Jorgensen never forgave her for hating bowling because bowling put food on their table. And she never forgave *him* for making her spend her whole childhood renting out bowling shoes. But really it's a tragedy of misunderstanding because there is a lot of love there if they could just let go of the past. And Mr. Jorgensen used to have a wife, but she died about fifteen years ago and everyone cried because she was a nice lady. And Mr. Jorgensen and the evil daughter have hardly seen each other since then because the wife was the glue that held the family together. Did you know any of that?"

Hank shook his head. "He never excavated any of that."

She explained why on Thursday. "*Apparently*, he doesn't like to talk about his family because it makes him too sad—at least that's what everyone thinks."

"It's making me sad too," said Hank.

"Yeah," said Maisie. "And my mom says that's probably why he loves his dogs so much, because his daughter is a real lemon."

On Friday, Maisie didn't say anything. She arrived late at school and slipped into her desk without even a smile.

By then Mrs. Vera was reading the book. Finally reunited, the boy and his faithful wiener dog, Leah, had made it back to the little hut in the woods after escaping another band of Nazi soldiers. They were surviving on dandelion greens and crickets now, but it wasn't looking good—and that was saying something since nothing in that book was ever looking good for anyone. Bombs exploded all around the boy and Leah at night. The rumbling and shaking scared Leah half to death, but she was so thin and tired that all she did was lie next to the boy and tremble.

Hank didn't know how much more he could take. He was sure the next bomb would get the boy and Leah. He could practically see the house and everything in it exploding into a million tiny shards, and if the house exploded Hank knew for sure that the boy would explode too, so Maisie's arrival could not have come at a better time. He nudged her and gave her a smile. She sniffed and looked down at her desk. He took a piece of paper and wrote, "Where were you?"

She wrote back hastily, "Bad news about Mr. J."

Hank's heart sank. He pulled out his three rocks (obsidian, topaz, amphibole) and after careful consideration handed the obsidian to Maisie.

She took the rock and began to rub her thumb back and forth against its smooth surface.

At lunch Maisie told him what she'd learned. "*Apparently*," she said in a sad voice, "the police called the evil daughter after Mr. Jorgensen drove his car into the ditch. They told her they were going to send a special checking-up-on-people person to make sure he was okay, and so she had to come with her prissy, yappy dog to figure out what to do with him before the checker-up person tried to put Mr. Jorgensen in a retirement home. And the 'current thinking'—that's what my mom calls it—is that Mr. Jorgensen will have to go live with his daughter in Minnesota.

"When my mom told me that"—she slumped forward—"I couldn't even finish my breakfast." She took the obsidian from her pocket and handed it back to Hank. "But then my mom said, 'Come heck or high water I had to pull myself together and go to school because she did not raise a moper.' But, I'm telling you, Hank, I feel mopey."

Hank's mouth fell open. Mr. Jorgensen moving? He didn't want Frank to move! He liked Frank. More than that, his moving would be like an earthquake. It would disrupt things and change things, and then what would happen? It was too terrifying to even think about.

Still, Maisie made him think about it. Looking across the playground, she said, "At first I thought, well, maybe Mr. Jorgensen will have to give us Booler and we can finally untie him from the tree. But then I thought that that would be a bad way to get Booler. And then I thought that maybe evil Colleen won't want to do us any favors, so maybe Mr. Jorgensen won't give us Booler. But then what would happen to Booler? What would happen to Cowboy and Honey? I doubt that lady would let Mr. Jorgensen keep his three dogs with him in her home. She's the worst."

"Stop!" said Hank. He was about to tell Maisie that she was giving him a bad day, but he knew that wasn't right. It was Colleen. She was the one giving him the bad day. A determined look on his face, he said, "We're not going to put up with this."

Maisie squeezed his arm. Her cheeks turned pink. "Yeah! We're not putting up with this one bit."

After school they went to Maisie's. They watched from the porch as the evil daughter pointed two men holding trash bags to a great big dumpster that had appeared in front of Frank's house.

Maisie shook her head. She rested her elbows on the porch rail. "That's not a good sign."

"Yeah," grumbled Hank. "This is making me as sad as the book. But we're still not putting up with this. Right?"

From Frank's backyard they heard Booler howl. Maisie and Hank frowned and nodded.

Maisie grimaced. "I didn't want it to come to this, but Mr. Jorgensen's daughter leaves us no choice. We are going to have to seriously butter that lemon up."

Hank squirmed as he imagined a lemon covered in glistening, greasy butter.

"That's right," continued Maisie. "We're going extreme. Extreme nice. Follow me."

They walked toward the tiny house and tried not to look at Booler when, upon seeing them, his howls turned to pleading whines.

"Slap a smile on, Hank," Maisie whispered when they

were near Frank's daughter. "And follow my lead."

He showed Maisie his biggest grin.

She stopped, a look of alarm on her face. "Well, that's just terrifying. Can't you just . . . you know . . . ?" She smiled widely.

"That's what I'm doing," Hank said, pulling his mouth so wide that he could feel the spring breeze on his gums.

"No. Like this, with your eyes too." She smiled again.

He looked at her eyes. They were open wide and her eyebrows were slightly arched. He strained to open his mouth even wider and to raise his eyebrows as high as they could go.

Maisie licked her bottom lip. She took her hands and cupped Hank's face in hers. Her fingers pushed down on his forehead. Startled, Hank blinked, his eyelashes grazing the palms of Maisie's hands. Then she turned his head slightly sideways. Her fingers slid down his face and she pinched his jawbone between her thumbs and forefingers and gently pulled it down. She let go, leaving her hands hanging for a moment in front of Hank's face, which now felt less tight and forced.

"Just . . . stay like that, okay?"

He nodded and they walked once more toward Colleen and her dog. Maisie started to wave.

"Yoo-hoo," she sang. "Hello there. I don't believe we have been formally introduced. I am Miss Maisie Huang and this is my associate, Mr. Hank Hudson. It is truly our pleasure to meet you."

They were standing near the woman now. Hank watched Maisie from the corner of his eye and tried not to change the expression she had arranged on his face.

Maisie reached out to shake Colleen's hand, but the little white dog gave an angry yap and the woman turned her body sideways as she ran her free hand soothingly across the dog's body.

Maisie's arm trembled and then dropped to her side. Maisie looked at Hank, who shrugged, his face still unchanged. She cleared her throat and tried again. Bright as a daisy she said, "I do declare, that is the prettiest, sweetest dog I have ever seen, and I went to a verrry fancy dog show in Santa Monica—that's in California—once, so I know what I am talking about."

Colleen's nostrils gave a little quiver. So did the dog's. "I'm sorry, but I'm really in the middle of something here." As she spoke her face kind of sagged and her lips kind of grumped.

Undeterred, Maisie asked, "What breed is your lovely pooch? I told my, associate, Hank that it must be a miniature poodle because the cutest little white dogs are always mini poodles, but he insisted it was a Maltese."

Hank nodded enthusiastically, his eyes wide, his smile still frozen in place.

Maisie's hands made a flopping gesture. "I said, 'Really, Hank, don't be ridicu—'"

"She's a poodle," the woman said, interrupting. She repositioned the dog so that its head looked over her shoulder. She began to pat the dog's back. "But like I said, this is not a good time."

Maisie jutted an elbow into Hank's side. "See, Hank? It's just what I thought."

From the backyard came the sound of a sharp, urgent bark.

Hank turned to see Booler straining at the end of his rope. He looked at Hank with a happy, eager face.

Maisie kept on talking. "I'm always right when it comes to dogs, and I'm absolutely obsessed with miniature poodles. They are the smartest, prettiest, most accomplished of all dogs. Don't you agree? I bet she has a pretty name too."

The evil daughter sighed. "Princess Lillikins—Lillikins for short."

Princess Lillikins began to squirm. She yapped, "Mrat, mrat, mrat."

Hank watched as Booler dropped his forepaws and gave another short bark. Hank pulled gently on the bottom of Maisie's shirt.

Maisie looked over at Booler, who jumped straight in the air and then—meeting the limits of the rope—fell awkwardly on three paws and whined.

Maisie bit down on her lip. "Um . . . so . . . can Princess Lillikins do any tricks?"

Hank's smile left his face. "Booler really wants us to visit."

Maisie rested her hand on Hank's arm. "The poor little sweetheart really does miss us, but what we want more than anything is to hear about adorable Princess Lillikins."

Hank started to talk but Maisie squeezed his arm. Hank pulled his arm free and took a step toward Booler.

Maisie pushed out her lips and put on a baby voice. "You are the sweetest. Oh, yes, you are the sweetest little Princess Lillikins. Aren't you?"

The dog squirmed even more and began to toss its head left and right. Throwing a nervous glance back at Booler, Colleen said, "Hold on." She placed Lillikins on the sidewalk. Pointing her finger at the poodle, she commanded, "Stay."

Nervously at first, but then with real determination, Princess Lillikins moved off the sidewalk and began to scoot under the lowest fence slat and into the backyard.

Booler dropped his front paws and wagged his tail.

Relieved, Hank pointed and said, "Look! Lillikins and Booler want to play. We can watch them while you do your work!"

Maisie clapped her hands. "That is happy family news! And we are happy to help!"

Colleen scooped up Lillikins. "Well, that is not going to happen."

Hank stiffened. He chanced the *a'a* feeling and looked the woman right in the eye. "But Booler is a good dog. Your dog will like him."

Maisie squeezed Hank's arm once more. "What my associate, Hank, means," said Maisie, a tremor in her happy voice, "is that Booler is always so gentle and kind and loving. I'm sure Booler would not hurt Lillikins, if that is what you are worried about."

The men came by—each holding another big trash bag—and Colleen stepped forward. "Wait, I thought you were going to bring out the boxes from the guest bedroom next."

Without saying a word, the men shuffled right past.

Colleen let out a garbled "pah" and raced to catch up with them. "Excuse me, I'm talking to you."

"Um," said Maisie, keeping close to Colleen's side. "Are you cleaning out your dad's junk? That's probably a good idea, huh? Because it is very crowded in there." There was no longer a tremble in her happy voice but there was definitely a strain.

"Yeah," said Hank, bringing up the rear. "And we already threw away the big knife, so you don't have to worry about that. And your dad gave us each a fossil, so that will clear some space too."

Colleen stopped, swiveled around. Her eyes had grown large. "Wait. What's that?"

Hank looked down at the ground. He could kick himself. For sure the evil daughter was going to want the fossil back now.

Colleen's eyebrows were knit together. "You threw a knife away? Why would you do that?"

"No reason," said Maisie quickly.

"Because he almost chopped his finger off," said Hank, grateful that Colleen hadn't asked about the fossil.

Booler began to bark again.

Maisie smiled. "Ummm . . . you're very busy. We'll just go calm down Booler for you." She motioned for Hank to climb over the fence with her.

"What do you mean he almost chopped his finger off?" Colleen clutched Lillikins closer and stepped toward them.

"We were just trying to help," said Maisie, climbing the fence and sounding perkier than ever.

"The knife came *this* close." Hank held his thumb and forefinger a half inch apart. "We really saved the day there. It wasn't like when he burned himself."

Booler began to bark even louder.

Maisie grabbed hold of Hank's shirt and whispered, "Stop talking. Come with me."

He nodded and began to climb over the fence as Maisie stage-laughed. "Booler, you are barking like crazy! You really should not be so bossy, you little pumpkin-sweetie-pie. We'll just come and calm you down right now."

"Yeah, we'll come and calm you down," repeated Hank as they ran to the pit bull.

The evil daughter leaned her back against the fence and let out a long, deep exhale. She put Lillikins on the sidewalk and began to rub her temples.

Lillikins did not hesitate this time. She wiggled under the fence and began to run to Booler, who dropped his head as the little dog came and sniffed his butt. And then Booler began to sniff Lillikins's butt. And then the two dogs walked in circle after circle sniffing each other's butts.

Maisie leaned in to Hank and whispered, "You can't tell her about the knife and the burn and stuff. Otherwise she'll make Mr. Jorgensen move for sure."

"Oh," said Hank, a sudden pang in his belly. "I didn't know."

"It's okay," said Maisie. "Just—"

"Princess Lillikins!" shouted Colleen.

Hank, Maisie, Booler, and Lillikins froze as Colleen went round to the gate and let herself into the yard. She marched toward them and swooped up Lillikins. Then she glared at Hank and Maisie, her cheeks turning jowly, her chin turning wobbly. "I told you those two can't be together." Her voice got louder and she added, "And, frankly, I did not give you permission to come back here."

Hank looked at the ground. Yelling always tempted the *a'a* feeling. He felt his breath grow short. He felt the prickly-dense feeling pull at his insides. He cast a glance at Booler, who was cowering in place, his tail thrust against his belly, his neck low, his eyes worried.

"In fact," said Colleen. She paused a long moment and added, "I think you should go. I have a lot of work to do here."

Booler's feet began to dance up and down. He shook his back and started barking again.

Maisie took a step toward Booler. "It's all right, Booler," she said calmly. "I got this."

She faced the woman. "You," she said, "are mean. You are an evil grouchpuss who does not deserve our buttering up."

Colleen held up a hand and started to speak, but Hank cut her off.

"That's right," he said, absorbing Maisie's confidence and letting it sweep away the *a'a* feeling. "And just because Mr. Jorgensen ran into a ditch and can't read the sports section doesn't mean he has to move." He shook his head. "How Mr. Jorgensen ended up with a lemon like you is a big mystery."

Maisie beamed at Hank. "Yeah, a big mystery!" repeated Maisie. She looked again at Mr. Jorgensen's daughter. "And miniature poodles are not the best dogs in the world—mixed breeds are!" She stalked off a few steps and then turned around, fixed her gaze on the white dog, and shouted, "Although you are very cute and definitely not as evil as your mama!"

"And you definitely don't deserve to have Booler named after you!" Hank yelled at Colleen.

Colleen staggered backward, a look of surprise and bewilderment on her face. She clutched Lillikins tighter than ever and the dog let out a strangled, confused "roo-oof."

Then Hank and Maisie stomped back to Maisie's house, where they stood on the porch, their elbows resting on the railing, witnesses to the evil daughter's rule.

Booler stared at them from the end of his long rope.

Maisie shouted, "Don't worry, Booler! We've got your back!"

"And you're going down, lady!" yelled Hank. "You're going down because we—me and Maisie—are the heroes of this story."

Good news arrived the following week. Colleen had gone back to Minnesota—at least for a while—and Mr. Jorgensen said they could play with Booler whenever they wanted. In fact, he told Maisie that she and Hank could have played with Booler the whole time if they had only asked him and not his daughter.

So of course they went over to see Booler and Mr. Jorgensen after school. When they arrived, Booler gave them such a tail wagging and such a tongue licking that Maisie finally had to say, "Booler, enough! Who knows where your tongue has been?"

They had barely wiped Booler's slobber from their faces when Frank rolled out to the yard with a plate of crackers and slices of American cheese. "I know you like the ham and cheese sandwiches," he said, "but I can't find my cutting knife anywhere, and whole sandwiches just seem too big for a snack, don't you think? It's probably those darn 'professional cleaners' Colleen hired. I can't find anything since they came through."

Maisie and Hank glanced at each other.

Frank held the platter in front of them as all three dogs gazed at the food, their expressions mingling greed and hope.

"About that . . . ," sighed Maisie.

"We threw it away," said Hank, taking a cracker. "When you almost chopped your finger off. We thought your evil daughter probably told you." He bit into the cracker and began to chew.

Teetering just a little, Frank lowered the platter into the basket of his walker and then went and sat on the little seat. He rubbed his face with his hands and made a long "auugggg" sound. A swirl of emotions passed over the old man's face until his shoulders fell forward and he started laughing. He laughed and laughed like he had just heard the funniest, saddest joke in the world. Then he took a deep breath and wiped a trickle of tears from his eyes.

Hank and Maisie looked at each other, worried.

Frank expelled a few more desperate chuckles. Then he shook his head and said, "I appreciate your concern, kids." He turned to Maisie and added, "But please do not do anything like that again."

Maisie and Hank both nodded.

He grabbed his knees, looked up in the tree. "You two have definitely made my life interesting."

"We're sorry," mumbled Maisie.

Hank looked at the bottom of the aggressive walker. "We didn't want you to hurt yourself."

"I've been hearing that a lot lately." Frank's face was red from laughing so hard, but his expression had turned serious. He got up and slipped a cracker to Booler while Cowboy and Honey went to sniff the toolshed. Then he stretched his arms high above him, and when he started to wobble he quickly grabbed his walker. He began to roll his walker around the yard, stopping every few paces and sighing.

Hank got up and began to stroll next to Frank. He finished another cracker and said, "We were only trying to help."

Frank nodded, took a few more steps, sighed once more.

Hank reached out and gently tapped Frank's elbow. "I'm sorry your daughter is a lemon."

Frank squeezed Hank's shoulder. "She's not a lemon. This is just hard for her—for both of us."

Hank nodded sympathetically. "Because she hates bowling even though it put food on the table?"

Maisie walked over to them, her hands folded together and tucked under her chin. "Mr. Jorgensen, you just have to let that go. Not everyone wants to spend their childhood renting out bowling shoes."

Frank scratched his chin slowly. "What are you talking about?"

"We heard all about it," said Hank. "And how you fought in a war, but not the one with Nazis."

Mr. Jorgensen looked at them with baffled eyes. "This is hard for Colleen because she has her own life and problems, and she just didn't expect to have to deal with this." He squeezed the handles on his walker tight and added, "Frankly, neither did I."

Cowboy and Honey came and sniffed at the platter of crackers and American cheese. Frank shooed them away, and with a loud smack of his lips he said, "It's nothing to do with the bowling alley. That was years ago." He pushed the walker a few paces forward and repeated, "That was years ago." Then he turned back and looked at them. Irritated, he said, "And for your information, I was never in a war."

"You weren't?" said Maisie.

"No." Frank tilted his head. "I did manage a recreation center for soldiers for a few years." He sat down again on the seat of the walker and rubbed his nose. "That's actually where I got the idea for the bowling alley. The rec center had one."

Cowboy came and dropped his head on Frank's lap. Frank began to massage the dog's neck. He got a faraway look in his eye and smiled. "Funny story: One day Bob Hope came by. He was visiting the troops. This one kid had broken his leg falling out of—I don't know—I think it was a helicopter. Had a full leg cast. He had to hop to the bowling lane on one leg while balancing a bowling ball—and he still beat Bob Hope." He shook his head and chuckled. "Bob Hope was the worst bowler you've ever seen in your life."

Hank smiled and said, "Who is Bob Hope?" and for a minute it seemed like Maisie's neighbor might laugh-cry all over again.

Hank looked at Maisie, who was wiggling a little, like she had to pee. She was holding her hands behind her back, twisting them. She seemed to be doing everything possible to prevent words from falling out of her mouth, but finally the dam broke. "I hate to say this, Mr. Jorgensen, but I think that maybe this wouldn't be so hard on your daughter if she weren't so snobby. She won't even let Princess Lillikins play with Booler. She's all, 'My poodle is too good to sniff butts with your pit bull.'"

Frank chuckled again. "That's not it." Cowboy moseyed away and Frank stood up. He brought his walker back over to Booler and sat down again. "Colleen breeds miniature poodles, and Booler isn't fixed yet. I'm hoping we can get his seizures a bit more under control before the operation.

Colleen just doesn't want any Lillikins-Booler puppies running around."

"Oooh, but they'd be so cute," said Maisie, coming over and rubbing her forehead against Booler's.

Booler sighed and dropped onto the ground. He closed his eyes as Maisie began to rub his belly.

Hank looked around. There was a softness to the day. A gentle blue sky. A whisper of a breeze. Everything that could be green in Mr. Jorgensen's yard was green. The trees were full of leaves, the ground was full of grass and weeds. And except for two lilac trees awash in purple blossoms and surrounded by an army of bees, everything seemed safe and constant and perfect. But it wasn't. It was all in flux. It could all change on a dime. At any moment! And it did! It would! A car could go into a ditch and lead to a hundred unexpected, horrible consequences. A pit bull could befriend a poodle and lead to the unexpected, wrong yet adorable puppies. Here they were, Mr. Jorgensen, Colleen, sucker punched by change—even the possibility of change—as much as Hank ever was.

Hank went and stood next to Frank. "I don't want you to move."

Frank took a deep breath. His shoulders rose up to his ears as he explained that he really did not know what was going to happen. He really did not know what was best for everyone.

"That's making me scared," said Hank.

A sigh escaped Mr. Jorgensen's mouth and his whole body seemed to shrink. He began to push his walker around the lawn once more. "Let's not think about that then."

So Hank tried his best not to think about it, until cruel change socked him one good.

What happened was this: Three days went by, and then Maisie showed up at Hank's house after dinner. She was sweaty from running and she had a long scrape on her arm.

Hank's mom swooped in close to her. "Maisie, are you okay?"

"I'm fine. I just tripped. Can I talk to Hank?"

Maisie pulled Hank into his bedroom. "The evil daughter is coming back. She's bringing a big U-Haul. She called my mom to ask if Cowboy and Honey could stay in our yard while they empty the house. And my mom said, 'Well, what? Is Mr. Jorgensen moving?' And she said, 'Yes. He'll live with me until we can find him an assisted-living home,' and so my mom said, 'And what are you finally going to do with the dogs?' And the evil daughter said one of her grown-up kids was taking Cowboy, another was taking Honey, and that she was taking Booler since Booler has special needs, and that she was going to tie Booler up to her own tree. But I heard my other neighbor say that that wasn't true at all. The evil daughter really wants to put Booler to sleep—she wants to kill Booler. She says he's too much trouble for her dad and for her."

Hank's knees buckled and he collapsed onto the carpet. In his mind he saw Booler alone, cold, still, sleeping an endless sleep. "That's the worst thing I've ever heard."

She sank down next to him. "Now's the time, Hank," said Maisie, grasping his shoulder. "Now is the time that we have to be strong, that we have to save the day."

"But how?"

"I've figured it out." She let go of Hank, went and peeked out his bedroom door. Then she closed the door, crawled inside his closet, and motioned for him to join her. She slid the closet door until there was only a sliver of light to see by and whispered, "We've got to run away with Booler. We've got to go to the forest—just like the boy."

Hank balked. "From the book! No way. Never." But even as he spoke part of him was still imagining an everlasting-sleeping Booler.

"Don't you see?" she said in desperation. "It's the only way. The boy went to the forest to hide from the Nazis. We've got to go to the forest to hide from the evil daughter."

"But . . . what?" The forest—all its darkness, all its unknowns, all its most terrible of unpredictabilities—descended on Hank.

"It's the only way to save Booler. We're the only heroes Booler has. It's up to us to save his life."

Hank started to breathe more quickly. *Save his life? Save his life.* The words echoed in his brain. He stammered, "Forever?"

"No, no." She tapped her elbow against his as she turned to face him in the closet. Half of her face still in shadow, she added, "Just until they're gone, just a few days. Then we can come back and no one will be able to hurt Booler ever again."

Hank didn't answer for a while. *Save his life.* The Booler in his head stirred. Its tail gave a little thump. "And then what?"

"Then . . . he'll live with one of us. We'll figure it out. And he won't be *less* anymore. And he won't be tied to a tree." She bit on her thumbnail. "But it will be sad that we can't say good-bye to Mr. Jorgensen."

Hank pushed open the closet door and let the light shine on them. He crawled out and lay on the floor. He looked like he was getting ready to make a snow angel. *Save his life.* "How soon?"

Maisie spread herself out next to him. "Whenever she gets here . . . a few days maybe?"

From outside Hank's room came the sound of Sam talking. Sam had learned the word "that," which he pronounced "dat," and now he kept repeating, "dat, dat, dat," to which his mom kept replying, "Which? This? This? This?"

It confused Hank. How could his mom and Sam act like everything was normal when, in fact, everything had turned all wrong? Squirming, Hank said, "Maybe we should talk to Mr. Jorgensen. Maybe he could tell her no."

Maisie nodded, her face screwed up tight, but then she said, "But what if he tries to tell her no and she's all, 'You have to do what I say because I'm the boss now and if you live in my house you have to live by my rules'? My parents try that one on me all the time. Plus, you know how much she wants to keep Booler and Princess Lillikins apart. No. I'm sure of it. She'll never let them live together. She said as much."

Hank tried to let that sink in; he tried to let it all sink in. Maisie got up.

"I've got to get home because my parents don't even know I'm gone." She looked down at him. "Don't worry. We can do this."

She turned to leave, but at the last minute she bent down

and whispered, "And, Hank, don't say a word! If anyone learns what we're up to—wow—it will be curtains for sure for Booler."

He heard the front door close and his mom walked into his room. "Everything okay?"

Hank turned over so that his face was shoved into the carpet. He didn't say a word. But he was thinking. Oh, boy, was he thinking. *Save his life. Save his life. Save Booler's life.*

"Well," said his mom, her voice wavering a little, "I'm here if you need anything." She leaned against his door for a minute. When Hank still didn't answer, she walked away.

Hank kept it together. He did not know how he managed, but he did. He walked to school the next day—slowly—as stiff as a board. He didn't even notice it, but he had begun to hum their favorite song. His gait grew a little looser. And soon he had begun to sing, "Do, do, do, do. 'Oh, we could be heroes, just for one day.' He stopped. *Just for one day.* Just one day. Or a few days. In the forest. It wouldn't be so bad. It was nothing he hadn't done before—except that his parents wouldn't be there. That made it completely different. His belly turned to ice. The refrain from the song looped in his head once more. He thought, *But we could be heroes. We can save a life. We can save Booler's life.*

He got to school just as the class was entering the

classroom. He ran to the back of the line and took his seat.

Maisie was ready for him. She passed him a note.

"Well? What do you say?"

In a firm hand he wrote back, "We are the heroes of this story. It's time to save a life."

She read the note. From the corner of his eye he watched as she tried to hold back a smile. She glanced at him for a second and then wrote some more. She slid the new note to Hank. "I've figured it all out. Meet me at the back fence at lunch. Now eat this note so no one finds it."

Hank crumpled the note and held it in front of his mouth. He glanced dubiously at Maisie, who frowned, grabbed the note, and shoved it into her own mouth.

When lunch came they raced to the back fence. Maisie bent down. "Pretend we're looking for rocks," she said. "Spies could be anywhere."

He got on all fours and began to rake through the gravel.

Maisie copied him. She whispered, "Okay. The most important thing is that we need to steal Booler, but if we are going to steal Booler we also need to steal his medicine, because if he doesn't have his medicine he'll for sure have seizures—and he hates those most of all."

Hank sat back on his calves. "Hold on," he said. "So, we are the heroes of this story, but the problem is that stealing is against the law. People who steal go to jail. So, you know, I'm not gonna steal anything. No way."

Maisie sat back. She brushed her hair out of her face. In a soothing voice, she said, "We're not really stealing. We're rescuing. We are rescuing Booler, but we can't rescue him without taking his medicine, right? And we can't be stealing his medicine because it already belongs to him. Get it?"

Hank stood up. His right hand did a lazy circle.

"What's the big deal? You took Mrs. Vera's book and set the bathroom on fire. This is way less than that."

Instead of winning Hank over, these words disturbed him even more. His hand began to circle faster. He remembered what he had promised his mother in the aftermath of the boys' bathroom disaster. No starting fires and no taking things that did not belong to him. Only now, only in that moment, did he realize that taking and stealing could actually be the same thing. He had already stolen. He had stolen Mrs. Vera's book. He had tried to steal Booler once before. He had already committed actual criminal acts. He could have been put behind actual bars. He felt a lump in his throat and he suddenly felt that he was actually behind bars, not prison bars, but invisible bars, bars that tightened around him, limiting the possibilities of that very moment. Uncertain how to respond, his body followed his spinning hand so that all of him circled round and round.

He said, "Um, I'm not allowed to take things that don't belong to me. It's one of the rules."

She began to jog next to him, but backward so that they were still face-to-face. "How about this?" she said, starting to pant. "I'll get the medicine. I'll get Booler. You don't have to take anything."

He spun a minute more and then stopped. He put his hands up to his mouth, pinched his lips together with his fingers. He let go of his lips. "So," he said, staring at the ground. "I won't be stealing anything. I'll just be heroing."

"Exactly."

A soccer ball raced by them, then two girls, and then three more girls.

The bell rang and Maisie said, "We'll talk more after school. I'll come to your house, okay?"

It was more than okay. Hank was keeping it together—he was even pre-heroing—but he needed time to absorb it all. Soak time. A lot of soak time.

"We're gonna need camping supplies," said Maisie. They were sitting on Hank's front steps. Hank's mom had made them do their homework—which had blessedly stretched

Hank's soak time even more—and now she'd given them Popsicles as a reward for their hard work. The melting Popsicle juice threatened to slide down Hank's arms and so he had begun to bite quickly into the frozen juice to avoid getting sticky.

"The good news," continued Maisie, "is that I have hiking shoes, a sleeping bag, and an actual canteen from back in the day when we used to camp. I can bring hot dogs, mustard, and marshmallows. I'm pretty sure those are the most important things. What can you bring?"

Hank fought off the *a'a* feeling. He closed his eyes and imagined that he was Mowgli, the boy from *The Jungle Book*. Mowgli was always brave and clever. Mowgli never felt pierced by sights and sounds. He never felt prickly and light and dense all at once. Hank thought of all the camping trips he'd made with his family. He thought of all the things they brought, used.

He said, "I have a tent, a sleeping bag, a tarp, a camping backpack with a mess kit and water bottle, a tiny emergency kit, a Swiss Army knife, a flashlight, a laminated guide to rocks and minerals, and a roll of toilet paper because sometimes there's no TP."

She paused for a moment. "Okay. Yeah. Those are good things too."

"I can make ham and cheese sandwiches and bring a can of peanuts."

Maisie wrinkled her nose. "I hate nuts."

"Peanuts are not actually nuts. They are officially more like peas."

She poked him in the shoulder. "So they're fake nuts, which is even more reason to hate them."

He poked her back. He needed her to see that this was not open for debate. "Mowgli likes peanuts when he goes camping."

"Okay, fine—but don't let me see them."

Maisie bit into her Popsicle. She glanced back at the house. Her voice barely audible, she said, "So here's the thing. We have to be ready by the time Colleen gets back. So just get all your stuff, and when I give the word, we go."

Hank realized he'd been holding his breath. He gasped and began to breathe again.

From the living room, Sam erupted into loud wails.

"I thought you babyproofed the TV stand," Hank heard his dad say.

"I did," said his mom, her voice fading as she explained that she had taken the padding off to get something from inside one of the cabinet drawers.

Hank blinked. "What if my mom asks?"

"Asks what?"

He shook his head and sighed. "Anything."

She placed a hand on his elbow. "Here's what you do. If she asks anything about Booler or Mr. Jorgensen, say, 'Just a minute, I have to go to the bathroom.' Then go to the bathroom and wait awhile. When you come back she'll have moved on to something else."

He tried it out. "Just a minute, I have to go to the bathroom."

"And sometimes—if she's not buying it—kind of jump around a little like you really gotta go. That even works on Mrs. Vera. I've done it a hundred times."

Hank repeated the phrase and nodded. He took a bite of Popsicle and got a brain freeze. It was the best he'd felt all day.

The first time Hank's mom found him in the garage he almost blew it.

"What are you doing?" she asked.

He was getting his sleeping bag from the storage unit, but he couldn't tell her that. He pulled at the hem of his shirt and glanced nervously around the garage.

"Hank," she said. "What are you doing?"

He remembered Maisie's advice and excused himself to pee. Then he ran out of the garage, and it was exactly like Maisie had said. He came back to find his mom chasing after Sam and that was that. It was like his mom had never spied him. He went back to the garage, grabbed his sleeping bag, and hid it in his closet. Then, feeling himself relax just a little, he sat in front of his bookshelf and began to say aloud his different kinds of rocks.

He was much better prepared when his mom found him checking his mess kit, and then when his dad found him counting his tent poles, and then again when his dad found him walking into his room with a big can of peanuts and his camping backpack.

"What's with all the camping stuff?" asked his dad.

"Just a minute, I have to go to the bathroom."

"That's it, mister," said his mom, watching from the other end of the hall. "You're going to the doctor."

She made an appointment for Monday.

When Hank told Maisie the next morning, she said, "Well, the jig will be up then. You can never fool medical science. But I don't think things will get that far. A real-estate van was parked in front of Mr. Jorgensen's house for a long time yesterday. Colleen will be back soon. And then . . ." She starting humming their song, but it was more than their song now. It was their code.

Hank gulped. "I'll be ready." He started humming too.

She shrugged. "You've got all your supplies then?"

He nodded. His hands wouldn't stop spinning.

His mom noticed it right away when he got home. "You nervous about something, Hank?"

He ran to the bathroom and frowned at the now baby-proofed toilet.

When he came back his mom shook her head and said, "I

really wish I could have gotten you into the doctor sooner."

It was definitely a *Jungle Book* night. Only Mowgli and Baloo could help him now. He sat on the couch, watched the movie, and talked in sync with the characters.

"You sure everything is okay?" asked his dad, wrapping an arm around him. "You seem pretty tense."

He murmured back, "The bare necessities of life."

"They'll come to you," answered his dad. "They'll come to you."

The phone rang and Hank's mom handed it to him. "It's Maisie. She has a homework question."

Hank hoped that that was true, but he knew it wasn't. He knew Colleen had arrived.

"Tomorrow," Maisie told him. "Just like we planned."

He swallowed and croaked, "Just like we planned." He hung up the phone and went straight to his room. He paced the floor and told himself over and over, "We gotta save Booler. Booler is my friend. Booler is counting on me. And Maisie too. And Booler gets so scared. And the evil daughter will kill Booler if we don't do something. And we could be heroes. Just for one day—or a few."

When he finally went to sleep he was clutching a framed picture of his family. He had not planned on bringing the picture with him. He knew that real campers travel light, but when he woke up in the middle of the night he shoved it into his camping backpack along with his sleeping bag and camping gear. Then, while everyone still slept, he made ten ham and cheese sandwiches. He stuck them in a cloth sack along with the peanuts and hid everything behind the bushes in the front yard.

He went back to bed and somehow managed to fall asleep—and stay asleep—until his mom came and got him. Then, like he was watching himself in a dream, he got dressed. He ate his breakfast, and when it was time for school he said good-bye to his mom, dad, and Sam and he left. He looked at his house one last time, collected his gear, and started walking.

He met Maisie halfway between their houses. That was the plan and that was what they did. Maisie was holding Booler by a leash that they had often used while walking the dog. She wore a purple backpack and hiking boots, and under one arm she carried Booler's water dish and his tug-of-war rope. "'Cuz you know Booler doesn't want to get bored," she explained.

Booler jumped up on Hank and licked his nose. "Good dog," mumbled Hank, a lump in his throat from how real this plan had suddenly become. "You're my friend. You're counting on me. Maisie too."

Maisie turned to face the mountain. "That the closest forest?"

Hank tightened the straps on his backpack. "It is."

"Then let's go." Her voice was serious and steely, like a superhero, and it helped Hank embrace his courage.

They walked for a while. Then Hank's head started to bob up and down. His sweaty hands on the straps of his pack, he sang, "Though nothing, nothing will keep us together—"

Maisie's shoulders rocked left and right and she joined in.

They sang for a while more. Then Maisie squeezed Hank's arm and said, "We are going to be heroes, Hank. Just wait and see."

They walked another block and Maisie said, "Hey, how long will it take to get to the forest anyway?"

Longer than they thought.

For such a close mountain it turned out to be pretty far away. After an hour of walking they were still on a flat plain surrounded by houses and yards, but eventually the houses thinned and the yards got bigger, and some yards now even had horses. Once, a horse looked over a fence at them as they walked by and Hank and Maisie were able to stop and pet it. Booler wagged his tail, interested in the unfamiliar scent and animal. The horse whinnied and Maisie laughed. She had never been so close to a horse.

They stopped and ate two of Hank's ham and cheese sandwiches, throwing their crusts to Booler and filling Booler's water dish and their own water bottles from a spigot they found near a stable. A few cows grazed nearby and Hank told Maisie about the dairy farm the class had visited in third grade. Everyone in the class had had a chance to pet a cow and three kids even got to try to milk the cow, but not Hank because he was not about to go anywhere near the underside of a cow.

Of course, Maisie said she would have jumped at the chance to milk a cow. "I wouldn't be scared. Animals love me."

The sun was high in the sky, and Hank and Maisie tied their jackets around their waists as they got ready to walk some more. They had grown tired of conversation and singing. Hank had grown tired period, and he felt it important that Maisie know that, so he told her frequently.

"We're all tired!" she finally yelled. She wiped her hair off her damp and sticky forehead. "But we have to keep going. So shush your face."

The street turned to dirt and they walked some more until it finally ended at a small ranch house. The house was painted forest green. It had a small, fenced-in yard full of freshly planted flowers. Beyond the house stood a detached garage. Outside the garage stood a gleaming black truck. But the most impressive part of the property was its nearby cow paddock. The cow paddock held about ten cows that were spread out in groups of two or three. These were the most animals they'd seen all day, a fact that Maisie delighted in repeating.

Beyond the paddock—they could see it with their own eyes—lay the tree-filled foothills of the mountain.

"We're almost there, Booler," said Maisie.

Hank shoved his camping bag and peanuts through the wide slats in the paddock and started to climb.

"Wait. What are you doing?" asked Maisie.

When he didn't answer, she said, "We have to go around."

"But this way is closer. And I'm tired. And my feet are sore."

"But that way is full of cows."

"So?"

"So they're . . . cows."

"You are lucky that animals love you," said Hank as he climbed over the fence, "because while it is an interesting fact that cows are gentle, the bulls can actually be mean and you don't want to mess with them. But this way is closer and my feet are sore and so I am done with this walking business."

Maisie gave a little whimper and followed him, first helping Booler through the slats of the fence. When they were on the other side, Maisie took the leash back from Hank and then, before he could say anything, she grabbed Hank's hand. "I don't think Booler likes those cows at all, so I think we should hurry through here and not get near any bulls."

Hank looked at Booler, whose nostrils crinkled and uncrinkled, and whose tail stood straight behind him. Hank, who had touched an actual cow at a dairy farm after all, adopted a little swagger. "Don't be scared, Booler. I only see the one bull. The rest are all lady cows and they won't hurt you."

They crossed the field in a zigzag pattern that led them as far away from cows and their giant lumps of cow poop as possible.

"It's the cow poop you have to watch out for," said Hank, feeling suddenly a little stronger as he realized how much he had to teach Maisie. "It's gross."

Maisie spied a small calf standing near its mother and sprang toward it. "It's so cute!"

A low, blustery sound made them look up. The lone bull lowered its horns as it stomped its hooves up and down. Maisie quickly ran back to Hank and grabbed his hand once more.

"I told you," said Hank, puffing out his chest. "You don't want to mess with the bull."

They left the paddock and entered the shady slopes of the forest, which seemed to go on and up forever. Pine trees and other green and growing things stretched high into the sky. At the first clearing—from one angle they could even see the cows—they pitched their tent. Well, Hank pitched the tent while Maisie held Booler's leash and watched. Hank could have asked for help, but he was still enjoying the authority he had won through his easy rapport with cows. Besides, he liked putting together tents. When he finished, he unzipped it with a flourish.

"Ta-da!"

"That's like a real tent you put together," Maisie gushed. "That's not like a toy or anything."

"That's because it is a real tent," said Hank. He took their belongings and stowed them in the tent. Then he zipped it up again and pointed a bossy finger at Maisie. "Never leave the tent open, otherwise you get bugs."

She nodded meekly. She took a deep breath, opened her arms wide, and looked up at the sky. "It smells like Christmas trees."

"We should start a fire," said Hank. "That's what we do after we put up the tent."

"Cool! Then it will really smell like Christmas. You come in here, Booler," she said, leading him into the tent. "You take a nap."

She zipped the tent carefully and joined Hank in gathering wood and piling it downwind of the tent. "Don't take sticks that are green," cautioned Hank. "They make too much smoke."

"Okay."

"You do it like this," he said, showing her how to stack the wood just right and circle it with a ring of stones.

"Okay. Wow. You're like the king of camping, Hank."

He threw back his shoulders, proud. He *was* like the king of camping.

"This is going to be so much fun," she said. "I wonder if anyone has figured out we're gone. I bet they have. I bet they are all, 'Maisie and Hank are gone. And Booler too. Our selfishness has driven them away. If only we had let them adopt Booler in the first place. Will we ever see them again?'" Maisie threw herself dramatically across the forest floor as she acted this out.

"They will," said Hank confidently. "In a few days." He was already imagining trekking home—back through the cow field, back down the dirt path, happiness blooming at the very thought of resting in his own bed and re-counting all his rocks. His heart gave an extra thump. He had only brought three rocks—the rocks that day. What would he do tomorrow? Reuse the same three rocks? That wouldn't work. But then he realized that he was in the forest. There were lots of rocks. Each of the few days he could find three new rocks. And then he could add those rocks to his rock collection. And so that would actually be a hidden bonus of running away.

"A few days. Or maybe a week. Until we know no one will hurt Booler."

He stood very tall and pulled on his collar, which suddenly started to feel itchy. "A few days means a few days— not a week. You promised."

Maisie sat up, dusted the dirt off her jeans. "Sure, a few. Or whatever."

"A few! Two nights. Three days."

"Exactly. Starting tomorrow."

He came and stood right over her. His voice as unbreakable as any rock, he said, "Starting today."

She screwed her mouth into a tight little ball and then let out a dramatic exhale. "Fine," she said, throwing her hands in the air. "Starting today."

Hank gave a brisk nod. Then he picked up one last rock for the firepit and put it down. He sat next to her. "You can start it."

"Fun!" she squeaked. "Give me the matches."

He looked at her like she was the silliest thing he had ever seen. "I'm not allowed to have things that start fire."

She turned to face him, her eyes wide. "I never said I was bringing matches."

"I didn't either."

He watched as the features on her face turned purple and slid toward each other, and it almost seemed like a volcano was forming right under her lips. But then suddenly her mouth deflated and her shoulders fell forward. "Well played, Mr. Boy Scout."

"I'm not a Boy Scout. Those kids get too loud."

She looked back at the firepit. "I guess we can have the hot dogs cold. And the marshmallows."

Hank stood. His hand began to spin. Then, as if they had been waiting for just this moment, his hunger and fatigue pounced on him so that all he could feel were hunger, exhaustion, and the absolute requirement for a campfire. "We always cook the hot dogs—on a stick. The marshmallows too. The stick makes it fun."

She jumped up. "Hey! We can try to start the fire the old-fashioned way, like with two sticks or—"

"Flint!" said Hank, yanking himself away from disaster as he pulled his three rocks out of his pocket. "I actually have flint! It's one of the rocks I brought. You can use it to start a fire." He showed her a gray rock shaped a little like an almond.

"Your rocks are saving the day, Hank!" She jumped in the air. "Hooray for rocks!" Then she ran over to Hank. "How do you do it?"

"I think it works like the Survival 4000 Fire Striker with Compass and Whistle. You bang the flint with . . . with . . . I can use my Swiss Army knife!"

"You figure it out. I'll get the hot dogs."

He rummaged around for his Swiss Army knife. When he found it, he flipped open the blade that doubled as a flat-head screwdriver and started banging it against the flint, gripped tightly in his other hand. But it wasn't working. It wasn't making a spark at all. He kept trying.

"Booler, no!" screamed Maisie.

Hank turned, stumbling over the pile of firewood. The flint flew out of his hands in a wide arc, disappearing into the forest floor. "My flint!" he shouted, scrambling toward where he'd seen it land and searching the ground, the *a'a* feeling bubbling up inside him.

He heard Maisie and Booler bound forward. "Look at this! Look at this!"

She shoved a plastic wrapper in front of his face. He pushed it away. "My flint."

"Booler ate all the hot dogs. All of them. And the buns. That was our dinner, Booler. Bad dog. Bad dog!"

Booler, ears perked up, barked once and, finding his tug-of-war rope, grabbed it with his jaw, tail wagging.

Hank fell backward. "You can't camp without hot dogs." The *a'a* feeling bubbled higher. It spread out to his arms. It inched its way up his throat. His voice didn't even seem like his. "First my flint and now the hot dogs." His hands tornadoed and he began to walk in circles. "I want to go home. I'm tired. I want my mom."

"Ugh. Everyone knows you're tired!" she yelled. "I walked just as far as you. I'm just as tired as you. I'm just as hungry as you. You never think about that. It's always you, you, you."

Her loud voice assaulted his eardrums. The cool colors of the forest grew hot and sharp as needles. He dropped to the ground and squeezed his eyes shut. "You're making me feel bad." More sounds—a cawing crow, the padding of Booler's paws on the forest floor, the distant moo of the cows—landed on him like acid and every part of him grew heavier and itchier and more and more distant. "You're making me feel bad. You're making me feel bad. You're making me feel bad."

At first, he didn't notice the gentle nudges against his face and sides, but then a heavy weight descended on his torso and legs. It was warm and soft and its heartbeat kept time with his. Like a heavy magnet collecting metal shavings, the pieces of his body seemed to return from wherever they had gone, reassembling into the boy named Hank. He became aware of a wet, gritty washcloth wiping his tears away, but—no—it couldn't be a washcloth. He opened his eyes to find Booler splayed on top of him, licking his salty face. Hank blinked and Booler let out a hot-dog-smelling sigh and dropped his head onto Hank's neck. Hank ran a hand down the smooth silver fur.

He whispered, "Good dog, Booler."

Maisie had come and sat next to him. She said, "Um . . . are you okay?"

He sniffed and shrugged. He felt tired and empty.

She put her hand on his shoulder. He flinched and she moved it away. "Um," she said. "Just so you know, that was like a whale of a freak-out, but—you know—I get it. And, um, everything is going to be okay. I promise."

He released a long, ragged breath. "You say things that aren't always true."

She nodded for a second. "Only when someone's life depends on it. But things really are going to be okay, so your life doesn't depend on it, so I don't need to lie."

"I wish I was at home." A tear leaked out of one of Hank's eyes. Booler lifted his head and slurped it up.

Maisie sighed. She picked up a small stick and started drawing with it in the dirt. Hank could make out a stick-figure girl in a triangular skirt, a stick-figure boy next to her.

She said, "Is this a bad time to tell you that Booler also ate the rest of the ham and cheese?"

He sat up, brushed the dust off. "If I weren't so tired I would go home right now."

She put down the stick. "Don't say that. We still have the marshmallows. And the peanuts, even though I hate them more than life itself."

He sniffled again. "Why do you hate life?"

"What? Oh, it's just a saying." She went into the tent and came back with the paltry remains of their food. "Here, eat something."

She handed Hank a marshmallow and popped one into her own mouth. Booler sniffed and watched her, his eyes intently following her hand as she took another marshmallow and put it into her mouth. "Yeah, you've had enough, Sandwich Sneak. That's what I'm going to call you from now on. Sandwich Sneak."

After a moment of silence, Maisie spoke again. "We could play Jungle Book."

Hank shook his head.

"We could look for rocks," she suggested hopefully. "Or sing?"

Hank shook his head again. He missed his family, his bed, his parents' cooking. This was nothing like the camping trips he normally took. Those had a logic, a pattern. Hank pitched the tent. Hank and his dad made the fire. Hank's mom unpacked and then played her guitar and sang songs while his dad joked about what a bad singer his mom was. At night they looked at the stars and told stories. In the morning they ate bacon. In the day they played UNO or his parents read books while Hank looked for rocks. That was camping. This was unroasted marshmallows. He took a sip from his water bottle.

Keeping his eyes on the ground, he said, "I'm going home tomorrow."

Maisie didn't answer.

He said it a little louder. "I'm going home tomorrow."

She still didn't answer. He looked up. Maisie was staring straight ahead, her body stiff except for her mouth, which smacked open and closed, and one hand, the thumb and fingers of which were pinched together and pulling on her shirt. She turned her head and looked right past him like he wasn't there.

"Maisie? Don't joke, Maisie."

When she still didn't say anything he shyly reached a hand out and shook her arm. "Maisie?"

She pinched her shirt, smacked her mouth. Then Maisie blinked and her eyes became heavy lidded. She swallowed and mumbled, "Did my . . . Where will . . . Yesterday." She rolled into a ball, resting her head on her hands.

He shook her again. "Maisie, are you all right?"

"Tired," she mumbled.

He was not sure what was going on, but he did know that—in his family—there was no sleeping outside the tent. "If you want to sleep you have to go in the tent," he said. "Otherwise you might get nibbled on."

"Okay," she said without moving.

Marveling at this completely un-camperlike behavior, he brought Booler inside the tent and unfurled Maisie's sleeping bag. He roused her until she crawled into her sleeping bag and let him zip her inside. Not knowing what to do next, he watched her sleep as he munched on the peanuts that Maisie hated. He knew that eating in the tent was also against the rules of camping, but he just didn't care. Booler inched his way toward him, his eyes on the nuts.

Hank's eyes narrowed. "Just one," he said, putting a peanut on the nylon bottom of the tent.

It was not the normal camping way, none of it, and it scared Hank that he had no idea what would happen next. He pulled the framed picture of his family out of his backpack and crawled into his own sleeping bag. Then he clutched the frame close to his chest, and when Booler settled his long dog body on top of him he felt a warm wave of grateful. He tried to remember the names of all the rocks in his rocks and minerals collection. He reeled them off to Booler. "Adamite, amethyst, calcite, chalk, garnet," and sometime after opal and before turquoise he fell asleep.

When he awoke it was dark outside. Maisie was shaking him, her flashlight shining in his face. It took him a moment to remember where he was, and when he did, the *a'a* feeling pinched him.

"How did I get in the tent?" she said. "I don't remember coming in here."

Hank explained all that had happened.

Maisie sat back on her heels, letting the light from her flashlight shine on the top of the tent. "How long ago was that?"

He shook his head.

She sniffed and looked around the tent. "Did you at least give Booler his medicine?"

"I? What?" He squirmed in his sleeping bag. His voice defensive, he said, "You were supposed to be in charge of that."

"I said I'd *take* the medicine—and I did; I snuck in when

that realtor van was there—but I didn't say I'd *give* it to him."

She riffled through her backpack until she found a baggie of little white pills. She handed two to Booler, who just sniffed at them. So she grabbed a marshmallow and pushed the pills into it. Booler swallowed the marshmallow-wrapped medicine without even chewing.

She rummaged in her bag again and then looked over at Hank. "Well, I guess that's it. I guess you won't want to be my friend anymore."

He sat up in his sleeping bag. It had grown cold, so he pulled the sleeping bag up round his chest. "What are you talking about?"

"You saw! And now you know that I have seizures too."

Confused, Hank's eyebrows slid toward each other. "But Booler is the one who has seizures."

"We both have seizures."

"But you didn't shake like Booler."

She took the flashlight and began to shine it in her bag as she shuffled everything around. When she spoke she used a very Mrs. Vera voice, one with no highs and lows, just plain and matter-of-fact. "My seizures are different than Booler's. Seizures can look different. That's a fact. But we both have epilepsy. And no one wants to be friends with people with epilepsy. People just want to tie us up to trees and make us live alone, and not take us camping or let us go on sleepovers because 'what if we don't get enough sleep and then have a seizure,' even though I might just have a seizure any old time so why does that matter? Or they want to walk behind us in the halls and whisper, 'seizure, seizure, seizure.' Like they're rooting for it to happen."

She dragged her hand across her crying face and then pulled a days-of-the-week pillbox from her bag and chased a small handful of pills down with water.

Hank saw himself in the school hallway. He heard the people behind him whispering, "seizure, seizure, seizure."

He slid closer to Maisie, afraid and sad and every kind of lonely. "I don't want to do those things."

Maisie sniffed. "Why not? That's how it was at my old school. No one wanted to talk to me or sit next to me or invite me to their birthday parties because they were afraid to catch my epilepsy."

Hank's eyes bulged. "Can I—"

"No! No," Maisie assured him.

Hank looked Maisie right in the eye. "I would never do those things."

She cocked her head, her mouth a crooked line. "Really? That's what everybody else does."

He swallowed. "I'm not like everybody else. I'm different."

Her eyes swelled and her crooked line of a mouth shook

until all she could do was lie back down in her sleeping bag and let the tears slide down the sides of her face.

What could Hank do but do the same? He lay next to her, his hand in hers.

He said sadly, "Can we go home tomorrow?"

She sniffled, sighed, and said, "Do whatever you want, Hank."

He listened to her sniffle some more. He listened to the sounds of the night—wind, an owl, a raccoon or skunk shuffling past the tent. He felt a lot of things, most of which were so knotted together that it was impossible to know what they were, where they started, where they ended. But he did know this: There was definitely shame involved. It was the way she said, "Do whatever you want, Hank." That was the clue. He'd heard that tone before—in his mom, when she really wanted him to do something and he just wouldn't do it and so she just finally gave up, disappointed, annoyed.

But surely—after everything that had happened—going home was the right answer. Wasn't it?

The shame poked at him. He could almost hear his mother say, "Are you being a good friend, Hank?"

But what did she know? She wasn't stuck in a tent with a crying Maisie—never in his life did he think he'd see a crying Maisie! A crying Maisie was like a crying lion. It just didn't happen.

Until it did.

He should have known. That's what he began to tell himself. A good friend would have known. At least twice he'd seen Maisie fall asleep for no reason—once up at Two Medicine Lake, once at her house. He hadn't even thought about it. And then earlier—when she'd been pinching at her clothes and then fell asleep again—all he'd cared about was that she was trying to sleep outside the tent. It hadn't even occurred to him that something was really wrong. She was his best friend and it was like he had never even seen her at all. A good friend would have seen her.

He pulled his sleeping bag higher. He had not seen her, but now he did. And he was the hero in this story. He would not let her down.

II.

Morning light flooded the tent. It was the longest Hank had ever been away from his mom and dad. He had dreamed of them. They had been eating pancakes and laughing about something silly Sam had done. He could almost taste the maple syrup when he opened his eyes. But then he knew. There were no pancakes. There was no Sam, no Mom, no Dad.

He wanted to be home. He wanted it more than anything.

He turned his head and saw Maisie watching him, her legs crossed, her eyes still puffy from crying. Booler sat next to her.

She said, "I know you want to go home, but just listen for a second." She began to fidget with the strap of her backpack. "You know how the sad book makes you all 'Ack! I can't stand this anymore'? That's how I feel when I see Booler tied to that tree. You don't know what it's like. You don't know how scary it is to have a seizure, to wake up all alone and confused, or to suddenly see a bunch of people looking at you all terrified—like *you* hurt *them*, like *they're* the ones suffering." She looked up, shook her head. "It's not okay. So this is me burning down the bathroom. I'm not leaving. I'm saving Booler. I have to." She shrugged. "Because we're the same."

"You're . . . You're not Booler."

"I feel like Booler," she said simply as she petted the resting dog. The light streaming through the tent had cast her skin a bluish color, making her look tired and a little sickly. "And if people can keep him tied to a tree or put him to sleep because he's too much work, then what does that say about me? What could people do to me?"

Hank crawled out of his sleeping bag and slid next to her.

"But no one can do those things to people," he said firmly.

"The Nazis did. And there are even places now where things like that happen." She unzipped the tent and, holding Booler's leash, got out. She looked down at Hank, her hands on her hips. The sun was behind her and he had to squint to see her. "So I'm staying. And I want you to stay too. But if you've got to go, then fine. Booler and I will take it from here."

Booler stretched and went and stood next to her.

Hank got out of the tent. He looked her right in the eye-brows and said, "I *see* you."

Maisie nodded. "That's because I'm right here."

Hank lifted his chin. He looked around the campsite. "We're gonna need food."

Maisie's head snapped toward him, a shocked look on her face. "You're staying? Really?" Without warning, she wrapped her arms around him. A new energy warmed her cheeks as a smile burst from her lips.

Booler let out a happy bark. He lifted himself onto his back legs and began licking their faces.

"I have an idea," said Maisie, leaning into Booler's kisses. She walked over to the little clearing, the one with the view of the cow paddock.

"I was thinking about it before you woke up," she said. "I thought about the book, and I thought maybe we could survive on nuts and berries, but you know I cannot abide nuts. Then I thought—ha! The answer is staring me right in the face, or rather, right outside the tent." With a dramatic flourish she pointed to the cow paddock.

Hank looked at the paddock, perplexed.

Maisie made her dramatic flourish again. "Ta-da!"

Hank looked from Maisie, to the cows, and then back to Maisie, a blank look on his face.

"Remember the baby cow?" she said. "It's got to have

a mama, right? And if there's a mama, there's milk, and if there's milk we can drink it, and if we can drink it we won't be hungry because my mom says milk is basically liquid chicken. We can survive on milk and marshmallows . . . and your disgusting peanuts. And maybe—if we can find them—berries. Isn't that a genius idea?"

Hank frowned. He knew now that he had an easy rapport with cows, but he was quite certain that this was not a genius idea. "I'm not milking a cow."

"I'll milk it," Maisie assured him. "You just have to tell me what to do. You saw kids do it, right?"

Hank screwed up his face, trying to remember. All he could tell her was that hands had gone under a cow, milk had come out in a thin stream, and—when they'd had a chance to take a sip—the milk surprised him by being warm.

But none of this flustered Maisie, who just answered, "I can wing it."

She handed Hank the leash and made her way to the edge of the trees, where she crept down and looked from side to side before sprinting to the fence.

Hank was walking toward her—an eager Booler leading the way—when Maisie started to run back. The problem, she said, was that there was no way to tell which of the cows was the mama cow since all of the cows sort of looked the same except for the bull, which had horns, and the calf, which was adorable and small. Did Hank have any ideas?

Hank had no ideas.

She ran back to the fence and then just as quickly returned again. The other problem was that they didn't have anything to put the milk in. Did he have any ideas about that?

Hank had no ideas about that either.

But he did have other ideas, and he wanted very much to tell them to Maisie. For example, he wanted to tell her that her plan was a real stinker, that he was not at all convinced she would be able to milk a cow, that milking required more than just squeezing an udder—that much he knew. A person had to know what they were doing. A person who did not know what they were doing might get kicked in the head. But before he could say any of this, Maisie sprinted back to the fence once more. This time he watched her climb into the paddock and run halfway across the pasture before running back to him.

Panting, her face red, she said, "Another problem is I'm actually a little scared of those cows. So what do you think I should do about that?"

Hank thought they should go back to the tent and eat some more marshmallows. So they did. Afterward, they went ahead and finished the peanuts. Maisie ate her portion without complaint and they both looked on a little sadly when Booler inhaled his in one gulp.

"I'm still hungry," said Hank.

"We could look for berries?"

Hank did have a bit of expertise there. It was not unusual for him and his mom to look for wild huckleberries when they camped, but twenty minutes of searching with Maisie only left them both hungrier and crankier than before.

Maisie sighed. "We're going to have to get that milk."

Her plan was a stinker, but Hank had to agree—especially after he took the final sip from his water bottle. They needed that milk. Even if he had wanted to go home now, he would not have been able to make it, not without something to eat besides marshmallows, and definitely not without something to drink.

They crept down to the cow paddock, together this time.

"Did you mean it?" Maisie said.

"Mean what?"

"Are you gonna be my friend, even when we get back?"

He nodded.

"Remember that time I said you were my best friend?"

He pushed away a clump of tall grass and nodded again.

"Truth is, you're my first friend. I mean, I've had other friends but they weren't real friends because once they would see me have a seizure they wouldn't want to play with me anymore. They just watched me with scared eyes and stopped inviting me to their houses. At least it was that way in my old school. I was hoping no one would find out about my seizures here. But that never works."

He shook his head and, in a voice as solid as any rock he owned, he said, "I won't tell anyone."

Maisie rubbed her eyes and blinked. "You're really not a lemon at all, Hank."

They reached the paddock, Hank holding Booler's leash and Maisie holding the empty peanut container, which she had christened their new milk pail. This time they got lucky. The cows had spread out into groups of one or two, and by whose side did the calf cling? Its mama, of course. She was one of the smaller cows, brown with white spots—just like the rest—but with a narrow face and massive, drooping udders.

At the fence, Hank tied Booler to a post—"Just for a little bit, I promise," Hank told him—and followed Maisie into the pasture. Avoiding manure and the bull, they tiptoed toward the mother cow. He tried to channel the authority he had felt the first time they tromped through the paddock, but he just couldn't do it. As much as he knew the plan was necessary, he also knew how horrible it was. His stomach pinged and made a worried gurgle.

Suddenly, Booler started barking. They tiptoed back and settled the dog down, lest the people in the ranch house hear him and come and find them all. They set out again for the mother cow, but just like before, Booler started barking. And the more Booler kept barking, the more Hank's stomach pinged.

Finally, Maisie suggested that Hank stay with Booler and that she go on alone. Relieved, Hank rubbed his belly and waved her on. Then he untied the leash and stepped back from the fence.

He watched as, at first, the cows mostly ignored Maisie. A few of them swished their tails when she passed. Others moseyed to the other side of the enclosure. But all that changed when she got close to the calf. From across the pen, the bull looked up. It let loose a long snort of suspicion and leaned forward.

Maisie froze. When the bull made no further movements she took a slow sideways shuffle toward the calf. She took another step, then another. Then, her eyes still watching the bull, she reached out and ran her hand across the calf.

The calf's ears twitched.

The mother cow ambled away and the little calf trotted behind her.

The bull seemed to relax. It wandered over to a pile of hay and began eating.

Hank held his breath as, moving slowly, Maisie approached the mother cow and put her hand on its side. She stayed with the animal as it moved to a long watering trough, where it dropped its head and started drinking. The calf, now on the opposite side of Maisie, did the same.

The bull could certainly not see Maisie in her new position. Unfortunately, neither could Hank or Booler.

Booler gave a low whimper that sounded a little like a creaking boat.

Hank comforted Booler—and himself—saying, "It's okay. Maisie has this under control."

But he wondered if that was true. It didn't help that time seemed to slow down, that every second that he could not see Maisie seemed like a minute and that every minute seemed like an hour. And that was before the bull decided that it too wanted some water, before it began its unhurried stroll to the watering trough, before the mama cow made a sharp "mraaaw" sound and the bull's unhurried stroll turned into a trot. Hank watched in what seemed like slow motion as the bull lifted its head and made a beeline for the mama cow as the calf bolted away.

Hank watched the mama cow's hooves dance up and down.

The mama cow's head was bent sideways, toward where Maisie stood. It made another "mraaaw" sound and stepped away, exposing Maisie to both the bull and Hank.

The bull began to gallop.

"Move, Maisie," whispered Hank. But then he thought, *That bull cannot hear me. I don't need to whisper.* And then he thought, *What if that bull* could *hear me?* And then he had his own stinker of an idea.

His stomach jumped as he yelled, "Over here! Look over here, bull!"

The bull stopped. It turned toward Hank. Its eyes grew beady and its nostrils flared. Lowering its head, it charged toward him.

Before Hank could even think to move, Booler sprang toward the bull, all bark and spit. Hank pulled on the leash with all his strength as Booler clawed at the ground and tried to hurl himself inside the paddock.

"Booler, no!" yelled Hank. "Maisie!"

The bull careened toward them. Hank thought for sure the animal would stampede through the wooden slats, but then suddenly the bull tossed its head and turned away. Trotting back to the straw pile, it shook its shoulders and gave a doleful snort, as if it just wanted to forget the whole thing.

Hank held his breath, stunned. Then he saw Maisie. She was outside the paddock, running the length of the fence. Her face was red and glistened with sweat.

Panting, she said, "That was close. Wow. That was really close."

He looked at the empty peanut container dangling from one of her hands. She hadn't gotten any milk.

She swallowed and held up the container helplessly. Still panting, she said, "The mama cow kept moving." She held her free palm up like a crossing guard stopping cars. "But don't worry. I have another idea."

She took Hank's hand and they crept over to the house.

"Remember the black truck that was there yesterday? Well, look. From over here you can see that it's gone. I noticed it when I was avoiding getting killed by the bull. So maybe the people are all gone too, right?"

Hank peered at the home. It was a ranch-style house, one floor, with a detached garage. The backyard was neat and tidy with freshly planted flowers and a raised vegetable bed full of seedlings. A hose stretched across the grass from the side of the house to the raised bed.

"So what are you saying?" said Hank, looking at the hose. His stomach had begun to settle down and he suddenly felt very thirsty.

She put a hand on his back. "Well, now that I'm looking around, I'm saying that I think hose water technically belongs to everyone. I think that is a well-known fact, so if we filled our water bottles with it that would not be stealing. I know how you feel about stealing."

"And we can't live without water," said Hank thoughtfully.

"No," said Maisie. "We cannot."

They ran back to the campsite, got their water bottles, and returned again. They tiptoed over to the spigot, peeking in the windows of the darkened house as they moved. Then they turned on the water and ran to the end of the hose, where they filled Booler's water bowl and their own bottles. They drank the water in big thirsty gulps and filled their containers once more.

Maisie pointed to the raised bed. "Carrots." She squatted and looked at them more closely. "Hmm. I think it is also a well-known fact that things living in the wild—like rabbits and deer—get to take whatever they want from people's yards. And since we are living in the wild right now, I think it would be totally expected of us to take some of these." She pulled up a row of young carrots, each about the size of a stubby finger. She took the still-running hose and rinsed the carrots off. With a smile, she looked at Hank. "See, I told you it would be okay."

"I do like carrots," said Hank, taking two carrots and eating them down to their leaves.

"And look," she said, pointing to a tree near the garage. "Apples!"

Hank shook his head. "Those are crab apples. They're really sour."

She shrugged. "They might not be."

"They will be."

"We'll see about that." She dropped the carrots into the empty peanut container, letting the greens drape over the sides of the can. Then she put the container on the ground next to her water bottle and handed Booler's leash to Hank. She ran to the tree and began to climb. When she was near the top she pulled off two small green apples and shoved them into her pants pockets. Then she grabbed two more and rolled them into the bottom of her long-sleeved tee.

Her tongue was hanging out the side of her mouth and she was beginning to climb down the tree when a voice yelled, "Hey!"

Booler stiffened and barked just as Hank turned to see a barefoot woman wrapped in a big pink bathrobe. She filled the frame of the house's back door. Something seemed to jostle her and suddenly a German shepherd sprang forward, hackles raised, spit flying out of its wildly barking mouth.

"Max!" said the woman. "Kids, wait! Max!"

Maisie jumped from the tree, shouting, "Run!"

"We weren't stealing!" screamed Hank, turning round, tugging on Booler's leash even as the dog, barking, pulled toward the German shepherd.

Maisie raced past him. "We're basically rabbits!"

Booler leapt toward Maisie and he and Hank tried to catch up to the speeding girl. Running faster than he'd ever run before, Hank glanced back and saw the woman dive onto the German shepherd. But now there was another person, a teenager, his head swinging left and right as he tried to figure out what was going on.

"Back to the tent!" panted Maisie.

They reached the tent and threw themselves onto the ground as Booler paced back and forth, his tongue hanging out of his mouth. Maisie crept over to the clearing. "I don't see anyone," she said. "But our goose is really cooked this time." Her eyes flashed worry as she turned and looked at the campsite. "We gotta pack up. We gotta go."

"Home?" Hope filled his voice, but he knew—he knew before she even said, "Let me think"—that they weren't going home.

They tried to erase the evidence of their campsite. "It can't look like we were ever here," warned Maisie as Hank broke down the tent and shoved everything in his backpack.

"I *see* you. I *see* you. I'm helping you. I'm helping Booler.

I'm helping you, just for a few days," mumbled a frantic Hank as he tamped down the *a'a* feeling that rumbled inside him.

"We've got to go deeper into the forest," said Maisie, grabbing the rocks and wood from their failed campfire and throwing them around. "Somewhere they can't find us."

He strapped on his backpack and then let his hands spin round and round as he muttered, "I'm helping Booler. I'm helping you. I'm helping Booler. I'm helping you."

A voice came from the direction of the house. "Hank? Maisie?"

From the same direction but higher in the foothills came another voice: "Mayyyyy-zeeee? Haaaay-nkkkkk?"

"Oh, no!" Maisie squealed. "They know it's us."

"What do we do?" whispered Hank.

She bit down on her lip and tightened her grip on Booler's leash. Grimacing, she took a sturdy step toward the clearing. "We'll lose them in the cows."

Quiet as could be, they made their way to the edge of the clearing. They looked toward the house. They looked toward the paddock with the peacefully grazing cows. They looked at each other.

Suddenly, Hank wrapped Maisie in a big hug. He let go and they watched for a moment as the dog sniffed their legs and then glanced up at them with trusting, curious eyes.

"For Booler," said Hank.

Maisie nodded. "For Booler."

With ferocious courage, they dashed across the open field and made their way toward the paddock. Hank watched as Maisie helped Booler through the slats of the fence and then stumbled through the gap herself.

She looked back at Hank. "Hurry, Hank! Hurry!"

"Wait!" yelled the woman in the bathrobe. She was standing at the far edge of the paddock next to another man and woman, and all of them were staring at him and Maisie with open mouths.

From behind him came another voice: "Hank! Maisie! Wait!"

He threw himself through the fence. He didn't see Maisie trip but he heard her. He heard a great *thunk* and a squeal. When he turned to look she was already running after Booler, whose leash she had dropped. Booler ran straight toward the largest huddle of cows, and there was the bull—its front legs lifting off the ground; its piercing, sharp horns glinting in the sun; its bellowing snort trumpeting alarm. Maybe it was because Booler was never free, always tied to a rope or tethered to a leash; maybe he was just like Superman and had a secret talent. . . . Whatever it was, the dog was a bullet. Already Booler had passed the cows and the bull and was now almost at the other side of the enclosure. So Hank ran that way too, but not before glancing behind him to see now four people making their way through the fence.

"Maisie!" he yelled. "They're coming!"

She was about fifty feet ahead of him and she turned when she heard his voice.

What happened next didn't make any sense at all. Maisie stopped and her eyes got huge and her jaw dropped so that her mouth was a saucer.

"Hank! Watch out!"

Suddenly, Booler sped straight past Hank. The dog circled round him, ending on Hank's left. Bark after bark erupted from Booler's mouth as spit flew across the pasture in angry bursts. It was an urgent bark, a warning bark. Hank turned to see the bull charging straight toward him. It lowered its head and Booler's barking became a shrill yelp.

Hank saw only a shadow of Booler begin to sail across the sky before he gasped and realized that he too was sailing across the sky and that there was the most terrible pain in his side, so terrible that he couldn't even marvel at how fast the clouds passed before his eyes or how his breath seemed caught at the very bottom of his throat.

He landed in a pile of straw and manure. For a moment the smell pulled at his nose and he started to gag, but then the pain in his side knocked the stink out of his brain. He became aware of a warm wetness spreading across his belly.

He lifted his head, stunned. What he saw gave him such a shock that the why and the wonder of it all evaporated. It was Mrs. Vera.

She knelt next to him, her eyes on his belly. She pulled off her jacket, balled it up, and pressed it onto his stomach. "Well, you never do anything halfway, do you, Hank?"

"Ow," he said, trying to pull away.

"Stay put," she said. "We've got to stop the bleeding."

"Bleeding?" He lifted his head again and tried to look down his body but all he could see was Booler, seven feet in front of him, splayed out, silent.

"Yes. Bleeding. That bull gored you, Hank."

"Why are you here? Are these your cows? I don't think I like them."

Mrs. Vera gave a nervous laugh. "No, no. It's just . . . half the town has been out looking for you two." She pressed harder on the balled-up jacket.

"Ouch," moaned Hank.

"It's okay," said Mrs. Vera. "Just relax. An ambulance will be here soon."

"An ambulance? Am I dying?" The *a'a* feeling exploded and mingled with the pain in his body.

"Calm down, buddy. You're not gonna die."

"No, no," he shook his head. "I'm not your buddy. You hate me."

She pressed harder on his wound. Her voice pained, she said, "Now, why would you think that?"

Hank plopped his hand over his face, darkening the sky. Salt and sweat tingled his tongue. "I'm tired."

Mrs. Vera ran her free hand through his hair.

"No, no. Stay awake, Hank. Hank . . . Hank! Tell me, why do you think I hate you? That's a funny thing to say."

"'Cuz . . . ," he said, his voice starting to trail off. His side was *really* starting to hurt.

"Well, I don't hate you, Hank," she said, her voice becoming more soft and gentle than he had ever heard it. "I just don't want you to think that you can do less than you can do. I just want you to have a world of choices. Hank? Hank?"

"You're a real piece of work, Mrs. Vera."

Hank awoke with his mouth feeling dry and cottony. He remembered enough. He remembered the bull and Mrs. Vera. He remembered the ambulance ride and being wheeled on a gurney down a long hallway in the hospital. What he didn't remember was how he had gotten into this hospital room.

He thought for sure he would find his mom seated next to him, but it was his dad who was there, splayed out on a chair in his emergency room scrubs, his eyes closed. Hank thought maybe his dad was asleep, but then Hank sniffled and his dad's eyes popped open and his whole body popped up. He was at Hank's side before the sniffle even stopped.

Dad seemed to read his mind. "Don't worry. Mom's here. She stepped out to get some coffee. She'll be right back.

She's been here all night. Lots of people have been here. I had no idea you were so popular."

Hank blinked and looked around the room. From his window he could see the peak of the mountain.

Dad took his hand in his. "Are you all right? How do you feel?"

Hank tried to speak but the words came out a croak.

Quick as could be, Dad was filling a cup with water and handing it to him.

Hank took a sip and tried again. "Where's Sam?"

"He is at Maisie's house. He was worried about you. We were all worried about you."

Hank took another sip. He peeked at his dad through the corner of his eye. "And where's Maisie?"

Dad squeezed his hand. "Don't worry. She's okay. She's helping her parents look after Sam.

"She brought you this." He held up a rock that had been painted so that it looked a little like Booler's face. "And this." He showed Hank an envelope marked "For my friend, Hank."

Hank took the rock and turned it over in his hands. The *a'a* feeling started bubbling up as the image of Booler sailing through the sky came back to him. "Is . . . Is Booler okay?"

Dad pulled the chair Hank had first seen him in closer and sat back down. "The last I heard he was about to get a bucketful of stitches. I think people were hopeful. Did he really try to save you from that bull?"

The sight of Booler standing sturdy and strong in front of the charging bull flashed through his mind, and Hank realized that his dad was right. Booler had tried to save him. He had stood right in front of him and tried to bark the bull away, and when the bull kept charging, he did not back down. He shielded Hank with his own body. A wave of gratitude and sadness shuddered through him as he pictured Booler getting stitched up by a vet. He wanted to be with Booler right then. He wanted to pet the dog's smooth, warm fur and tell him that everything was okay, that he would love him forever and ever.

"We only wanted to save Booler from Mr. Jorgensen's daughter," said Hank.

Dad sat back. He clasped his hands together behind his head and sighed. "So I hear." He paused and then stood up and looked out the door. When he came back he said, "You know, your mom doesn't want me to tell you this yet—she's afraid you might . . . react poorly—but I gotta be honest with you. Mr. Jorgensen is pretty upset."

While his father was not using his angry voice, he was

using his I-am-very-disappointed-in-you voice, the same one he had sprung on Hank after the fire.

"You stole the man's dog, Hank. Again. Not just that, you stole that dog's medicine and his leash. And I know for a fact that you spent days planning this because I saw you with your camping gear. So this was not some rash, spontaneous mistake."

"I don't know what 'spontaneous' means."

"It means doing something without thinking. But it's my turn to talk right now: I'm not mad. Your mom's not mad either. We know your heart was in the right place and we're just glad you're okay. But Mr. Jorgensen feels betrayed. He thinks you were using him and that all you ever wanted was to take Booler, and not only did you take him, but you got him hurt."

Hank slumped forward. "You're making me feel bad."

His father leaned closer. He tried to catch Hank's eye, but Hank turned and looked at the mountain in the distance.

"Maybe you need to feel bad, bud. I thought we'd been through this. That's not how you want to be treated. That's not how you treat your friends."

Hank blinked and took another sip of water. His heart had been in the right place—Dad said so. He had tried to save a life, to do the right thing. Yet, somehow, it had been the wrong thing. He really did not want to think about Booler with a bucketful of stitches, or about the stealing he'd done, but he couldn't help himself. He was making himself feel bad. Maybe he needed to, like Dad said. Maybe that's what he owed Booler.

Avoiding Dad's gaze, he took the envelope that his father had placed on the bed. Inside it, he found a card from Maisie. On the outside, Maisie had drawn a picture of her, Hank, and Booler in front of their tent. On the inside it said, "Dear Hank: I hope you feel better. You are a good friend. Thank you for being the opposite of a lemon, which is, I guess, an orange. Thank you for being an orange! Ha ha . . . Orange you glad we're friends?"

Hank closed the card and rested it on his chest. He would have plenty of time to feel bad about betraying Mr. Jorgensen and getting Booler hurt, but . . . "Orange you glad we're friends?" How could he not smile at that?

Hank was in the hospital for one more day. Most of it was spent listening to his mom tell him how lucky he was that the bull had not hit any major organs, how fortunate it was that the woman in the bathrobe had heard about them running away and had alerted the police about their whereabouts, and how amazing it was that Mrs. Vera's volunteer search-and-rescue team was nearby when the police got the call. Then his mom would get weepy as she repeated that she—his mother, who loved him more than anything—had almost died of worry wondering where he was, and how he was not allowed to ever run away again, and how she was so, so, so glad he was okay.

He was relieved that she did not say the things Dad said, but he remembered those things, and every time he did he remembered Booler standing up to the bull. His dad was right. They had not saved Booler. They had nearly killed him.

"But he's doing much better now," said Maisie, who came to visit him the afternoon he got home from the hospital. They were in the living room eating some of the chocolate chip cookies she'd made for him. She'd also brought a big piece of obsidian, a gift from her parents. Sounding like she had a lump in her throat, she added, "And he—we—had an adventure. Right?" There was a lot going on in her voice. There were a lot of mixed-up and unnameable feelings there. He felt them too. He felt bad. And guilty. And who knew what else.

"Also," she said.

When she didn't say anything more, Hank looked over at her. She seemed very immersed in twisting the bottom of her shirt.

"Yeah?" he said.

"Also . . . I am"—she let go of her shirt, looked up at him; when he instinctively turned away she stared at his chest—"I am sorry that you and Booler got hurt. Really. That was scary."

He took another cookie and then stole a look at Maisie. "I'm sorry that some people are mean to you about your seizures."

She sat back, sighed. "I can deal with it."

Sam toddled by with a sippy cup, singing. Singing was his latest accomplishment. But he only knew one nameless and pretty tuneless song. It consisted of the word "bear," as in "bear, bear, bear, bear, bear."

Maisie turned to Hank suddenly. "Hey, guess what? You're sort of a superstar now—wait and see."

He was indeed a superstar. On his first day back at school he got to show the whole class his stitches. He could tell by the questions his classmates asked—"Were you scared? Does it still hurt? Were you really trying to save a dog?"— that they were impressed. More than that, he could tell they actually saw him—just like he had seen Maisie—and he liked what they saw.

"I've got some bad news for you," said Mrs. Vera that

same day. "We finished the book when you weren't here."

"That is not bad news," said Hank. "I hate that book."

"Is that right?" said Mrs. Vera, once again donning that completely unreadable half smile. She put a hand on his shoulder. "Well, it was a hard story. It had a sad ending. Some stories do. Sometimes we just do our best to endure."

Sadness tickled Hank's throat and he thought again about the sad ending he and Maisie had nearly given Booler. He slipped his hand into his pocket and fingered his rocks. They were new. In fact, he had a lot of new rocks. Maisie's parents had given him the piece of obsidian. His grandparents sent him a cool lamp made out of salt. Even one of the doctors gave him an old marble actually made out of marble.

But Hank was not a superstar with Frank Jorgensen, and neither was Maisie. Frank hadn't even answered the handwritten letters of apology that their parents had made them send him and Booler. And their playdates had been put on hold too. Maisie's mom and dad had put the total Cinderella on her, telling her that she would be cleaning their house for the next twelve years, exchanging her labor for Booler's veterinary bill, which they had insisted on paying. Hank's parents had liked the Huangs' cleaning idea so much that they put the total Cinderella on him too. Now when he went home he had to do all the annoying and boring tasks that his parents threw at him, including mopping the kitchen floor, cleaning out the linen closet, checking all the expiration dates on the canned food, sweeping out the basement (which he especially hated because it always somehow smelled liked boiled asparagus), and weeding the backyard.

It was several weeks before Hank's parents decided he had done enough cleaning and he had earned a break. School had ended. Hank and Maisie were official fifth graders, but Hank felt like a kindergartner heading off for his first day of school when he walked to Maisie's. He was excited, of course. He would get to hang out with Maisie. He would get to see Booler—maybe. Maybe not. That was all up to Mr. Jorgensen, who Hank still had not heard from.

Hank's feet became heavier with each step he took, and by the time he reached Maisie's his heavy feet were wary. What if Booler saw him and, instead of barking and wagging his tail in delight, he growled because he was so angry to see the boy who had gotten him hurt? What if the growling alerted Frank, who ran out with his aggressive walker and tried to roll over and squish him?

By the time Hank reached Maisie's he was sweating. He crouched down and tiptoed up the walkway to Maisie's house. When no barking came from next door he gave a sigh of relief. He was about to ring the bell when his curiosity got the best of him. He inched over to the corner of Maisie's house and peeked into Mr. Jorgensen's yard. He saw Booler's doghouse, but not Booler, not Honey, not Cowboy. No one was there at all.

Maisie explained. Booler and Mr. Jorgensen had left with the evil daughter that morning to check out the "assisted living options" in Minnesota. Frank had asked Maisie's parents to keep an eye on his house, as well as on Honey and Cowboy.

"I guess he doesn't trust us to take care of Booler, though," Maisie told Hank sadly. They were lying on the grass and looking up at the clouds. During his cleaning stint Hank had found a book about clouds. Reading it, he came to an amazing discovery. There were actually many interesting facts about clouds. He was anxious to share some with Maisie.

"Believe it or not," continued Maisie, "I think we kind of maybe might have been wrong about the evil daughter. I mean, of course, she is evil, but not so evil that she wanted to put Booler to sleep. She came right over here and swore that she would never do anything like that, that putting Booler to sleep would break her father's heart and, plus, make him really mad at her. Then she said that I should never listen to idol gossip, but I told her I'd been listening to my neighbors and didn't even have any idols, so I didn't know what the heck she was talking about.

"And I guess the vet went ahead and fixed Booler when he was at the hospital. That means Booler can't give Princess Lillikins puppies. Of course, now the evil daughter is all, 'La-de-da, look at what a sweet dog Booler is.'" Maisie groaned. "Like she couldn't have just seen that to begin with."

There was a clattering sound at Frank's house and Hank turned his head to see Honey and Cowboy trotting into the yard through the doggy door. They went and sniffed Booler's doghouse. Then they peed near the maple tree and began to circle the yard.

"I feel really bad about Mr. Jorgensen," confessed Hank.

"Yeah. We really bought the wrong cookies there."

"Wait. There were cookies?"

"I just mean we messed up. Big-time."

"Oh, yeah," said Hank. "Big-time."

He sat up and watched Cowboy and Honey go back into the house. He was reminded of how small and spooky he had first found the tiny little home, what with its peeling paint, one boarded-up window, and general air of disrepair. Then his gaze moved onto Frank's yard. Now that he really looked, now that he saw it not just as an extension of where he and Maisie might play, he could see how forlorn it was. The lawn was as much weeds as grass and there were large sections of just dirt, especially under the maple tree where Booler spent so much time. And much of the ground—green or brown—was covered with dead plants, small sticks, and twigs, and even pieces of trash that had fallen out of the garbage months ago and become part of the fabric of the yard.

"Mr. Jorgensen's house is making me sad," he said, standing up and looking again at the sad little house with the sad backyard.

"Yeah. It's making me sad too," said Maisie, pulling herself up next to Hank.

Hank put his hands on his hips. "I'm tired of it making me feel sad."

He crossed into Frank's yard, Maisie right behind him. He knew suddenly what he needed to do, what he probably should have done months ago, and he carried himself like the hero of a story, his spine straight, his jaw clamped tight.

"What are you going to do, Hank?" asked Maisie, following his lead for a change. She was jumping up and down and her eyes were shiny marbles. "You're not going to burn Mr. Jorgensen's house down, are you?"

"No." He shook his head, his disbelief coming out in a loud "pwww."

He went to the toolshed at the very back of the yard. He pulled open the door. The sudden light captured a scene sadder than the house itself. Abandoned garden and home-repair tools, all of them half covered in rust and dust, stood crowding one another at odd angles. Hank scanned the contents of the shed. He found an old rake and pulled it out.

"I'm going to make this place happy," he said.

With short, even motions he raked the backyard, creating small debris piles that Maisie transferred to big plastic garbage bags brought over from her house.

They began to hum their favorite song, belting out the refrain as usual, but then Maisie said, "I'm the boy and you're Leah. We survived the war and beat the Nazis. And now we are cleaning up our little house in the forest. Leah, can you believe what a big mess those evil Nazis left? Nazis are the worst."

At the mention of the book, Hank felt the lurking presence of the *a'a*. Yes. Nazis were the worst. Hank had no doubt about that. They had killed people just for being different. They had killed people like him, people like Maisie, people like the boy. But he had been thinking about something Maisie had said in the forest. It would not leave his head actually, not when he looked at rocks, not when he looked at clouds, not when he swept the stinky floor. She had said, *"What could people do to me?"*

Now that was as *a'a* a question as Hank could imagine. He knew bad people existed. But he figured that the best thing he could do was to not be like those people. He would keep being an orange instead of a lemon.

"Actually, I'm Mowgli and you're Baloo," said Hank, as Honey and Cowboy once again came outside and, spotting Hank and Maisie, raced over to say hi. "Honey and Cowboy are friends of Raksha and we are all cleaning up so we can throw a party for our wolf mom."

"Yeah. A welcome home party! Oh, Mowgli, Raksha will be so surprised."

"Yeah. And Mowgli is going to tell everyone interesting facts about clouds because he knows lots of them."

When they were done with the raking, Hank started weeding while Maisie reseeded the dirt patches of the yard with leftover grass seed she found in her garage. She had also found leftover seeds for tomatoes and cucumbers, so when they finished working on the lawn they turned the dirt in a little raised bed that looked like it had gone unused for years and they planted Frank a vegetable garden. Hank found some nice-looking rocks and, between rows of seeds, he used them to spell out "sorry."

Around lunchtime, Mrs. Huang yelled, "Hold the phone! What the heck!" She was standing at the fence with her chin tucked into her neck.

She said, "What are you two doing? Mr. Jorgensen didn't . . ." Her voice trailed off as her eyes scanned the raked and weeded yard and the turned ground in the once-neglected raised bed.

"Are you cleaning Mr. Jorgensen's yard?" She looked from Maisie to Hank. "Nice work."

She returned soon with a blanket and a picnic, which they ate in Maisie's yard while Cowboy and Honey, imprisoned on the other side of the fence, watched with fascination.

The next day they tackled the front yard, weeding, covering dirt patches with grass seed, and pulling out dead plants and replacing them with young flowers that Mrs. Huang got for them.

The day after that they swept Frank's porch.

The day after that they washed the windows, and when they reached the boarded-up window they talked to Mrs. Huang, who turned out to have the amazing skill of knowing how to replace a broken windowpane. How she'd kept that talent secret all these years was a mystery that boggled Maisie's mind.

Hank was not there when Frank and Booler returned home. He had gone camping with his family. They had a campfire and cooked hot dogs and marshmallows on sticks. Hank's mom played her guitar and sang, and Sam listened while Hank told him all about clouds. When they got back there was a message waiting for Hank. Mr. Jorgensen wanted to talk.

Uneasiness draped itself over Hank. It was not *a'a*, though. It was more like a Band-Aid that had worn its welcome. It was time to tear it off, and Hank was ready. He walked over to the little house with his mom and Sam.

"I'll be here if you need me," she said to him, hanging back with Mrs. Huang while Hank continued on to the house next door.

Maisie was with Frank when Hank got there. She was sitting on a camping chair near the doghouse. There was a chair set up for Hank. Frank sat on the little seat of his walker, Booler at his side. Cowboy and Honey sniffed the yard. At the sight of Hank, Cowboy and Honey trotted over. They sniffed at his feet and then flicked their tongues to lick his hands. Booler did not growl—that was a good sign. Instead, Booler walked as far as he could and waited for Hank to reach him. The dog lowered his head. His feet danced in place and his tail flopped back and forth.

"Hey, Booler," said Hank, his body instantly relaxing. "Good boy. Good boy." His eyes fell on a long scar that cut across Booler's silver fur. Hank felt a sudden lump in his throat, but the pit bull lurched up, rested his paws on

Hank's shoulders, and began to lick Hank's face.

"Booler!" exclaimed Hank, happy again. "I missed you too, boy."

When Booler settled down Hank took his place in the empty camping chair. He looked over to where he had left Sam and his mother, but they had gone into Maisie's house. He looked at Maisie, but she was looking at her lap. So he looked at Frank's forehead. Then his mouth. He didn't chance his eyes.

"I'm sorry for everything," Hank said.

Frank's mouth twitched. He said, "I appreciate you saying that, and I appreciate how much you care about Booler. But that's not why I asked you here." His mouth twitched again. He swallowed and said, "I wanted to talk about the things you two did to my house."

His house? They had only tried to make the house happy. The uneasiness that had begun to lift itself off Hank returned, heavier this time.

Hank shook his head. "No, no, no," he muttered. "The house was so sad."

Frank cleared his throat and dropped a hand onto Booler's head. "I wanted to thank you for sprucing up my home. You did a nice job. Even Colleen was impressed. It was a thoughtful thing to do."

Hank pulled his rocks out of his pocket (orthoclase,

hyalophane, olivine). The polite words that had come out of the man's mouth did not match his voice, which was serious, very serious.

"You know, I really don't want to move. I love Meadowlark. Always have. My life, my friends, are here."

"We don't want you to move either, Mr. Jorgensen," said Maisie, copying her neighbor's tone. "And not just because of Booler, but because of you. We like—"

Frank held up a hand and Maisie stopped talking.

"While I appreciate all the work you did over here, it— well, it and some other things—made me realize how much I've stopped doing, how much is now hard for me to do."

Maisie began to wilt. "Does that mean you're moving to Minnesota?"

"Well, even a few days ago I would have said yes, and to be honest I was getting kind of used to the idea." He leaned back in his seat. "Turns out you were right about Colleen. She's got some anger that's been building up for years. Since the bowling alley." He shook his head. Then he chuckled. "But she loves that I named Booler after her. Whichever one of you shared the gem, thank you." He slapped his thighs and added, "The point is, we've been talking and, well, I guess it's good to talk."

"It's always good to talk," said Hank. "Not talking stirs up the *a'a*."

The wrinkles between Frank's eyebrows deepened into a puzzled V. He cleared his throat. "But now I've been thinking."

Something about the quiver of that last word—"thinking"—made Hank look up.

"If I had some helpers, if I could find some do-gooder type people who could help me keep everything in order—"

Hank stood up. "Us! Choose us! We are do-gooder types of people."

"I'd have to pay, mind you," said Frank. "I'd need to know that you would come regularly and that you would do the things I needed—and not just the fun stuff either."

"We can do it, Mr. Jorgensen. We would be happy to do it." Hank plopped his rocks back into his pocket and his hands began to spin, but they didn't spin in the *a'a* way, not in the destroyer-of-worlds way. They spun because he could not contain his happiness.

"And if I could find someone—someone who lived very close, mind you—who could share with me the work of taking care of three dogs—"

"Mr. Jorgensen," said Maisie, jumping up and down. "That's me, Mr. Jorgensen. I live very close to you. I would be happy to share that work with you."

"Hold on a minute," said Frank, pulling his back straight so that he stood tall on his seat. "There's something else that is important to discuss, so sit down."

Maisie sat down. Hank threw her a worried glance.

"All this help you're offering will be a blessing to me, but it won't help Booler. Here is the thing. I've spent too many hours at the vet with this dog. He doesn't like it. I don't like it. And I don't even have a car to take to the vet anymore. I know it is not ideal, but Booler is still going to need to stay tied up to that tree. It's the only way I've found to keep him safe."

The weight of Frank's words pushed Hank back down in his chair. He looked at Maisie. Her legs were curled underneath her and she looked like she would cry.

"I know that this issue is very personal for you, Maisie."

She looked at Frank, her neck darkening. "You do?"

"Sweetheart, your parents explained it all to me a long time ago."

She pushed her hair in front of her face and looked away.

Hank remembered the night in the forest. He remembered Maisie staring, her lips smacking together over and over. He had promised to keep her secret—and he had—but here was Mr. Jorgensen knowing it anyway. Hank pulled his chair close to Maisie and put his hand on her shoulder.

"I need to know that you will respect my decision," said Frank. "I need to know that you will trust me to know what is best for my own dog."

Maisie twisted in her seat. She peeked over at Hank and sighed. He could not tell what she was thinking. Her face was as much a mystery as Mrs. Vera's, but he felt somehow that she expected him to do something, say something. But what could he say? What could he do? He was not a planning genius like Maisie. He was not a hero dog like Booler. He looked away, toward Maisie's house. He could see Sam's stroller standing outside Maisie's front door, and if he tried very hard he thought he could hear his brother crying the way he did whenever he ran his face into a piece of furniture. Sam hardly ever cried like that at home anymore, what with all the babyproofing, but Maisie didn't have a baby in her family. Her house was a normal house with normal sharp edges and pokey corners. Leave it to Sam to figure that out so fast.

Hank suddenly had a non-stinker of an idea. "You should babyproof your house."

Mr. Jorgensen looked at Hank like he had just recommended brushing his teeth with cauliflower. "What the heck is babyproofing?"

Maisie's eyes grew wide. "Hank, you're a genius!" She jumped up and ran home.

"It's really annoying," Hank explained, watching Maisie run. "It is when you put a bunch of padding on the edges of your tables and furniture so that your baby brother won't break his head open if he falls."

Maisie was already running back, followed by her mother and Hank's mother, who held a pink-faced, runny-nosed Sam in her arms.

"Do you have more babyproofing supplies, Mrs. Hudson?" asked Maisie, a big grin spread across her face.

"I guess so," said Mrs. Hudson.

"And if it was okay with Mr. Jorgensen could you help put it all around his house so that Booler wouldn't hurt himself if he fell during a seizure?"

"Of course," said Mrs. Hudson, smiling. "If that's what Mr. Jorgensen wants."

Mr. Jorgensen looked from Hank's mom to Maisie to Booler. He shrugged his shoulders. "I guess we could give it a try."

Booler galloped across the long expanse of the yard. The time in the cow paddock had not been a fluke. The dog was fast. Superfast. So fast that Maisie and Hank had started playing The Flash. Booler was the Flash. Hank and Maisie were his trusty sidekicks. Cowboy and Honey were a rolling parade of evildoers, but they were always good sports about it.

Maisie and Hank had been true to their word. They were excellent do-gooders. They wrapped padding on all of Frank's wood furniture and duct-taped bubble wrap near everything in the yard that might be defined as pokey or sharp. They pulled Frank's trash bins to the street before trash day. They helped him dust his house and empty his dishwasher. They bathed and walked the dogs. They gave the dogs their flea medicine. They weeded the vegetable garden.

There were some things Hank and Maisie could not do. They proved horrible at cleaning bathrooms. They proved even worse at doing laundry. They could not take Frank to the doctor or cook healthy meals. But with the help of a couple that Colleen hired to come in twice a week and assist with the bigger jobs, things settled into a new normal, a normal that looked like friends helping friends.

Sometimes even Hank's and Maisie's parents got into the act, like when it came to changing the propane tank on the old grill found in the toolshed. And, according to Frank, if you were going to change the propane tank, then you should at least fire up the barbecue to make sure it worked. And if you were going to barbecue you might as well make a little party of it.

So Frank provided the hot dogs, and Hank's dad made some potato salad, and Mrs. Huang made a chocolate cake, and when Frank couldn't really read the writing on the barbecue knobs, Mr. Huang said, "How would you feel about me doing the grilling? Maybe you could teach me."

And—boom—the party started.

At one point Hank overheard Mrs. Huang whisper to his mom, "I'm not entirely sure how long this *solution* can last."

To which his mom replied, "Well . . . it's good enough for now."

Hank moseyed away. He didn't like thinking about what might come next, like if Mr. Jorgensen's eyesight got worse, or if he started to need a wheelchair instead of a walker, or if if if if if if. If there was one thing he knew about the word "if," it was that it could be really unpredictable.

So he went and waited next to the barbecue. Cowboy and Honey stood nearby, their eyes following each hot dog as it moved from the grill to a plate. But Booler was just running, running, running, every once in a while stopping next to Cowboy and Honey and nudging them with his nose, lowering his front legs and wagging his tail, and giving them each a sharp bark.

Come, he seemed to say. *Don't you know we are free? It's time to play.*

Hank had just scooped some potato salad onto his plate when he saw the SUV pull up. He recognized its Minnesota plates and looked around for Maisie. She was sneaking pieces of hot dog to Honey and Cowboy. He sidled up next to her and pointed at the car.

She grimaced and said, "What fresh bother is this?"

The two of them were actually getting along better with Colleen these days. A few weeks earlier she had come to help with a yard sale. The whole purpose of the sale was to clear out space in the little house. It had been Frank's idea, but on the day of the sale he started having second thoughts, saying, "You never know when you might need things." Instead of being a real pill about it, Colleen had listened patiently to her dad and didn't seem evil at all. But then she was also in a very good mood because Princess Lillikins was getting ready to become a mom to "perhaps the finest litter of miniature poodles the world has ever seen."

Maisie had smiled when Colleen shared that bit of news, but later she told Hank that "a lemon is a lemon."

Hank figured you could not argue with that logic.

They watched Frank roll over to the front fence that separated his yard from the sidewalk. He was nodding at his daughter, whose mouth was moving like a car on an open highway. Occasionally, he would look around until he saw Booler and shake his head.

"What's going on?" said Maisie's mom. Her arms were crossed and tiny wrinkles stretched down from her pinched mouth. She and the others had come to stand next to Maisie and Hank.

"It's Colleen," said Maisie. "Finally everyone's happy so of course she has to come and ruin everything."

"You don't know that," said Mrs. Huang, one fist now tucked beneath her chin.

Frank shrugged and walked over to them as the daughter returned to her car. "It turns out we have a bit of a Romeo and Juliet situation on our hands," he said, with a twinkle in his eye.

Hank tugged on his mother's sleeve. "What does that mean?"

She suppressed a surprised laugh. "I think it means Booler is a dad."

The back of the SUV popped open and now Hank could see a large metal dog crate strapped in tight. Colleen leaned into the back of the car and when she emerged she was holding four puppies. She brought them into the yard and settled them onto the grass, where each one raced in a separate direction. Except for possessing a ridiculous amount of curly white fur, each puppy looked exactly like a miniature Booler.

Maisie's eyes were bugging out. "Those are the cutest puppies ever!"

"He's the proud papa all right," said Colleen, trying hard not to smile as she headed back to her car.

Maisie tugged on Frank's shirtsleeve and whispered, "I thought Booler got fixed."

He whispered back, "I guess not soon enough."

Colleen returned holding Princess Lillikins, who tossed a lovelorn look at Booler.

Bottom line, there were four puppies who would need homes as soon as they were old enough to wean, and Colleen, in an unexpected gesture of goodwill, thought Booler and her father should at least get to meet the cuties before she began the hard work of finding them families of their own.

"And make no mistake," she said grumpily. "It *will* be hard, unappreciated work."

"I'll take them!" said Maisie, falling down in front of the puppies and cooing. "I'll take them all."

"You'll take one," said her mother and father at the exact same time.

"I'll take one! Hank will take the others," Maisie declared, with a quick flip of her hand in his direction, not taking her eyes off the puppies.

Hank froze, aware without looking that every eye was now on him. He had finally adjusted to a baby brother. He had finally adjusted to furniture covered in padding, and a scar on his side, and late afternoons playing The Flash, and pulling trash bins to the street. Could he handle three puppies? Would his parents even let him have three puppies? His mother had been very firm before. She had refused to let him have Booler, and Booler had needed a hero. Then Booler had been a hero—Booler had been *his* hero.

He looked at the little balls of fur with their stocky legs, square heads, and soft white curls. The other dogs, including Booler, had come up to them and were darting their noses close to the new dogs, taking a quick sniff and then pulling their heads back. They circled the puppies as if they weren't quite sure what to make of the little fluff muffins.

Hank's mom and dad squatted next to Hank. Hank's mom had her arms wrapped around Sam, who said, "doggy, doggy, doggy," and reached with frustration for the puppies beyond him.

"What do you think, Hank?" said Mom.

"You could have one, but it's up to you. It's really up to you," said Dad.

It would be so hard. It would mean turmoil and change and disruption, disruption, disruption. And what if the puppy was loud? And what if the puppy was wild? And what if the puppy knocked over his rock collection? And what if the puppy did things, things that Hank could not predict, that Hank did not like, that made him feel all *a'a*?

Hank looked again at the puppies. One stood alone. While the other three puppies turned their faces from dog to dog and person to person, happy tongues lolling, one puppy plopped its belly on the ground and began sniffing a rock.

Booler came and crouched next to the rock-sniffing puppy.

He nudged the puppy with his nose. The puppy pulled out a little tongue and licked the rock. Booler cocked his head and then licked the rock as well. The puppy looked up at Booler. Then it wiggled forward and put its head on Booler's paw. Suddenly all the puppies were next to Booler, nudging him, jumping on him—all but the first puppy. That one kept its head on Booler's paw and gave its tail a lazy thump.

A smile crept across Hank's face. He was ready to be a hero.

ACKNOWLEDGMENTS

Dear Reader:

Thank you for reading this book! Your engagement high-
lights the myth that writing is a solitary pursuit. It is not.
We Could Be Heroes was always written with you in mind.
Likewise, I relied on a team of earlier readers who gave
me ideas and constructive criticism so that I could revise
what I thought was a good book into a much better one.
Those readers included my daughters, Elizabeth and Mary
Finnegan. Elizabeth has autism and epilepsy, and she
helped me write—what seem to us—honest depictions of
those experiences. Mary is really good at finding holes in
logic and helped ensure that my story made sense. Cathy
Perlmutter, Jackie Sloan, and Desiree Zamorano also gave

me helpful advice about improving my work. After all those people read my story, I revised it, and then guess what? I got even more (and really good) feedback from my agent, Tracy Marchini. So I revised my story again! And then guess what? Tracy sold this book! So then I got more (and really fantastic) feedback from the editor at the publisher, the amazing Alex Borbolla. So I revised my story again. AND THEN AGAIN! AND THEN AGAIN JUST TO CHECK FOR TYPOS! So I want to thank all of these people—including you—because without everyone's help, this story would still be a nice rock in desperate need of polish.